To Mary E. Lizie

ONE
NEW HAMPSHIRE
Christmas

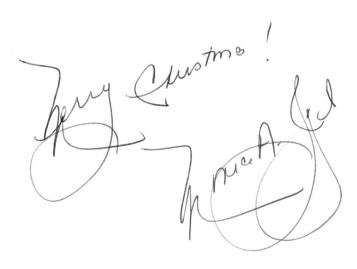

Merry Christmas!

Monica A. Joyal

MONICA A. JOYAL

Paperback ISBN: 978-1-09832-822-1
eBook ISBN: 978-1-09832-823-8

Dedication

This book is dedicated to the survivors
and descendants
of the Halifax Explosion in Nova Scotia, Canada,
on December 6th, 1917.
And to the evergreen spirit of Christmas.

What is Christmas?
It is tenderness for the past,
Courage for the present,
Hope for the future
—Anonymous

Gratitudes

When an author writes a book, they are never alone. I want to thank the Pawtuckaway Lake Improvement Association, and the literary club, Ladies of the Lake, for their care of the lake, ongoing support, and many friendships over the years.

A special thanks to Jeff Gurrier for sharing his wonderful interviews of past residents of the lake with all of us. There is no lake without those who love and protect it.

I also want to thank my husband, Wayne. Without his constant presence, my words would never have taken flight.

TABLE OF CONTENTS

PROLOGUE

Meghan MacNamara O'Reilly had one foot in Arizona and the other in New Hampshire. This was her third return trip to the Granite State in 2014. Her summer on Pawtuckaway Lake had opened her eyes to the multiple attractions that had drawn her father, Jack MacNamara, to settle there after retirement. His neighbors and community friends greeted her with open arms. A widow now, Meghan's own grieving heart had begun the process of healing.

She had planned to remain on the lake only till September. Fall arrived, and Meghan felt that the settling of the MacNamara estate was anything but finished. She may have found herself falling in love even! But with whom? A person or a place? Excavations of family memorabilia left her with a lot to learn. What had become of Jack's father, Will MacNamara? Did he simply succumb to the dangers of riding the rails in the 1930s like so many men?

And so, Meghan had to make her way back to Arizona where her tenants were forced to break their lease. Severe weather required repairs in her home there, but within weeks she had the place up and ready for new residents. On the first opportunity that she got, she was on a plane headed East. Destination-Manchester New Hampshire. She intended to celebrate Christmas with her children and grandchildren at the MacNamara camp on Pawtuckaway Lake.

1

Had the time finally arrived for Meghan to make her own decision? Did she really belong here and not back in Arizona? And what would it take for her to be sure of this?

Certainly, this would be a special and much-awaited holiday season in a camp nestled deep in the snow this one New Hampshire Christmas.

CHAPTER 1

———◆•◆———

"Home for Christmas"

The city of Manchester appeared like folds of white bedsheets to Meghan O'Reilly. She stared out from the plane. This time of the year, the windy line of the Merrimack River appeared snake-like against snowy banks. The rest were just lights.

It was clearly Christmas in New Hampshire, and the closer her plane came to the runway, the more her horizon became the lit streets and homes. The entire scene had been redrawn into a black and white photograph. The snow outlined and gave shape to most things.

While Meghan spent her weeks in Arizona repairing the damages to her home from the wind and rain, homes in New England were digging out of the Thanksgiving snowstorm of 2014. She had followed the weather reports closely, having flown out only hours before it hit. Some parts of the state were powerless for weeks. The sheer weight of so much wet snow in November had pulled down power lines, trees, and roofs. Landing at the Manchester-Boston Regional Airport on this December day only added more evidence to the occurrence of the snowstorm, with many hangers and unused runways blanketed still.

Meghan's stay in Arizona had lasted only long enough to complete the repairs and sign a lease with her latest tenants. They were a nice retired couple escaping to a warmer, dryer weather. Meanwhile, she could not seem to get back to the cold New Hampshire fast enough.

It was December 17th, just days before Christmas. She must have appeared rather mad to be heading East. The new tenants had said as much.

"Why are you leaving? Not that we aren't delighted to lease this lovely place, but isn't it very snowy there? Wasn't it just in a terrible snowstorm?" The elderly woman had asked Meghan while quickly signing their three-month contract.

"I have family there," Meghan had managed to explain, smiling brightly at them.

"And then there is the lake," she'd added softly.

"Pawtucket?" The husband had inquired.

He was friends with Meghan's Arizona neighbors and seemed to know something about her circumstances.

"Pawtuckaway," Meghan politely corrected him, "My family camp is there."

Her Arizona home was left in good repair. She felt confident in leaving it in the hands of this couple for the winter months. And so, after having sent a few emails to her lake neighbors, Meghan had packed her bags, purchased her tickets, and was anxious to head back.

Why the need to return? There was no simple answer.

All of this played in her mind as the plane landed and taxied down the runway. She was thinking straight. She even thought of bringing an extra bag containing woolen sweaters, a fleece vest, cotton turtlenecks, and sensible boots. She purchased a sharp pair of brown leather boots with her new down jacket. The jacket was the same color of cobalt blue as Sam's. It was packable. She recalled the one she'd borrowed on their last date.

Christmas, she mouthed. Her next stop was Christmas. She had two weeks to get ready. At the moment, she had no presents for anyone. She wasn't even sure who was on her list.

The Finches, next door to her father's camp, emailed that the power was back on at the MacNamara camp. They had been forced out for a few days, but the lake was back on. The roads were another story. She was advised to be sure to get snow tires immediately.

Like an Ansel Adams' photograph, New Hampshire's winter wonderland still inspired Meghan. What would any Christmas be without snow? The beauty of Arizona stood out in stark contrast with its brown landscape. . It was as if she carried the warmth of one state to the next. She had deep attachments to them both. But right now, snowy white days ahead felt so inviting.

"It's 18 degrees Fahrenheit in snowy Manchester," the pilot announced. "Welcome to our wintry state. Remember to put on hats and mittens. And thank you for flying Southwest Airlines."

Clicking metal sounds and movement filled the cabin as passengers unlocked seat belts and donned winter clothes. On the outside was a cold, gray scene, but on the inside, Meghan felt anything but cold. She shoved her gloves inside the pockets of her cobalt jacket.

"Home." These words left her lips.

An elderly man offered to help Meghan with her bag, but she assured him that she could manage. A young man smiled as he shoved arms into a vest covering a sweatshirt with the letters 'SAN DIEGO' spelled out on his back. A small package in colorful green and white fell from a woman's bag as she pulled it from the overhead bin. "I'll be home for Christmas," Meghan hummed as she followed the other passengers into the jetway.

CHAPTER 2

———◆◆◆———

"The Road Home"

No one met Meghan at the airport. Alice and Bob Finch, her lake neighbors, apologized profusely in their last email to her. They had some vehicle problems having slid on ice just days before. Their car was in the shop. Also, Bob had a doctor's appointment scheduled for four o'clock, the same time at which Meghan's plane was arriving. She would need to rent a car.

"Rent a large vehicle," a smiling woman behind the car rental desk had suggested when Meghan told her where she was headed.

"We highly recommend that to any customer heading up North or intending to drive on any country roads."

Meghan had planned to lease a compact, like she usually did, but went with the woman's advice. If Bob had faced trouble driving on the roads, she knew she would too. And so, an SUV came around and Meghan loaded it with her bags. It was bright red. She smiled to herself. Even her means of transportation seemed to be dressed in the holiday colors.

"My sleigh," she said as she jumped in.

All in all, the roads were in good shape. New Hampshire had a reputation for working miracles with their winter clearing and sanding. It was evident that the recent dumping had been a challenge. Not since childhood had the snowbanks appeared so mountainous. Unlike the greens of spring, the scene along the highway revealed forests of white, leaves still hanging on their limbs, and white birches bent over from the weight of the snow. Some trees had to be removed from the roads and could be seen pushed back along the roadside to allow cars to pass.

But Meghan was humming Christmas tunes.

"I'm dreaming of a white Christmas," she sang.

It was wonderful to be back. She wondered what shape her camp was in. The roof had held up, but was there leaking inside? Then there were the boats, neither winterized nor covered. She had thought that she would have more time to finish her fall clean up. Now, there would be leaves under the snow until spring. Her plans with the beach had gone undone. How could she be both in Arizona and there? The Finches assured her that there was nothing to be concerned about. Bob had raked the roof. Such an odd thing to do, but it was the only way to lighten the load on the structures.

The brown sign for the state park appeared as Meghan took a right at exit five. The familiar landmarks looked oddly out of place with snow-tipped poles sunk into snow banked supports. She spotted the Ben Franklin hardware store and made a mental note to get back there as soon as she could. She'd need a good winter shovel for starters.

Up the road a few miles, she spotted the big brown state sign for Pawtuckaway State Park. It too was iced in the snowy frosting. Turning left she anticipated her next landmark– the Mountain Road trading post.

"Happy Christmas, George," she called aloud to the popular owner.

She could see the red 'OPEN' sign encircled by an over-sized evergreen wreath.

It took only minutes to reach the dirt road leading down to the lake to her father's camp. She didn't plan to put up their name. He had not. It may sound silly, but it made their place on the lake a little bit of a hideaway. Anyone who knew them knew where to find them, Jack had always believed.

The lady at the car rental desk had not misled Meghan. The moment she hit the camp road, she was grateful for the size of her rental and its snow tires. The access road had taken a beating. The town and residents of the town had performed a yeoman's job to clear and sand the road, but she took her time. It was almost five o'clock, and the road was in darkness. She switched on her high beams but wondered if they only reflected against all the white. And with all the pushed back snow, recognizing twists and turns felt impossible. The topography was severely altered this time of year. Many times, she wanted to stop but told herself to proceed slowly.

Meghan encountered no other traffic on the road. It was very narrow, and she began to wonder where she would go if she met another car. Suddenly, a wave of unexpected panic rose inside. Here she was on a lonely dark road driving an unfamiliar SUV which hogged the space. She loosened the grip she found herself applying to the steering wheel, and took a deep breath. She had stopped singing.

"Silent night, holy night. All is calm," she began singing.

Her eyes strained to see the road over the next ridge. Did she detect headlights? Was someone coming at her from the other side? Carefully, she drove up. Something caught her eyes just as she reached the top of the hill. She saw a rock cairn.

In all her drives on this road, how was it that she had never noticed it before? Sure enough, there was a series of them at the curve of the ridge. She and Tom always looked for them when they hiked in the White Mountains. But here?

Cairns are left by fellow travelers. They are there to offer directions- to assure you that you are on the right trail. Someone had placed them there, like a lighthouse, except that they stood out darkly against a sea of white. Meghan's shoulders dropped. Her breath slowed. She felt calm. Tears welled up in her eyes.

She was not alone.

The camp would only be a few yards ahead. Rolling down her window by an inch, she breathed in the cold air. Her tires made a crunching sound beneath her. Down over the next curve, she spotted the green edge of the MacNamara camp rooftop. As she slowly took the turn and headed down the hill, the window above the kitchen sink came into view. A single white light shone there. Someone had left it on for her. An oasis in the snow.

Turning her car into the narrow driveway, it was obvious that someone had also cleared a place for her to park and had shoveled a path to the porch.

And there on the porch sat a small green tree lit with white lights.

Half laughing and still crying, she began to sing,

"Oh, Christmas tree, Oh, Christmas tree."

The season had begun on Pawtuckaway Lake. And she felt anything but alone.

CHAPTER 3

"A Fine Welcome"

The SUV came to a complete stop. Meghan shut off the engine. The hum of the heater went quiet. For a moment, she just sat and looked at the camp- apparently already prepared for winter. She smiled at the tree and the tiny light winking from the kitchen. Just beyond the building lay an ice-covered lake. Framing the view, dark limbs added a wintry touch to the scene. As far as the eye could see everything was white. She put her hands on her lap and took it all in.

She was finally here.

The Finches would be home soon. They said they should be back around supper time. Glancing over at their place, white lights shone from each window. Bob had rigged a spotlight and aimed it at the side of the house where an enormous evergreen wreath hung. All was white, black, and green. Such a contrast to the russet colors of arid Arizona. But just as breathtaking.

Finally, Meghan was ready to leave her warm SUV. She could barely squeeze through the door with the four-foot snowbanks piled up on both sides of the driveway. She wiggled into her new boots before disembarking, glad of her choice of flat-soled footwear. A solid footing with traction would make her headway inside much easier. The only noise in this muffled winter wonderland came when she pushed the side of the door as far as she could. It squeaked with resistance.

The light from the tree lit her way to the porch steps. She pulled her carry-on behind her. Crunching noises came from the luggage wheels as snow stuck to them. Up the steps, she pulled it, step by step.

"There, I made it!" Meghan said with a sigh.

She let go of the bag and turned to pull the porch door open; it too dragged in the coating of snow. From the corner of her eye, she thought she caught something move.

"Oh!" was all the came out of her mouth.

Meghan lost her balance and almost fell over, as the familiar shape of a furry animal jumped up on the porch, cried, and then ran back, running in circles. For a full minute, the poor dog acted as if Meghan had come back from the dead. Once again tears began to fill her eyes, but she found herself laughing so hard, she landed on top of her own suitcase.

Exhausted, Max, Jack's golden retriever, ran back up on the porch and sat before her, his wet tongue lapping her face furiously. She wondered which of them was happier to see the other.

"Max, you crazy dog. I sure have missed you! Sorry I was gone so long. But I'm back."

She rubbed his sides vigorously as the dog groaned with pleasure.

What better greetings could there be?

CHAPTER 4

———◦—◆◦◆◦◆—◦———

"Lights in the Window"

Some semblance of order was returning to the Pawtuckaway community and the Granite State. The Thanksgiving snowstorm that had so disabled much of the Eastern coast was in a major clean-up mode. But mostly, residents merely chose, as Yankees do, to get on with it.

Ed Shea was no exception.

His roof rake leaned against the shed, and his shovel sat idly by the back door. A bucket of sand overflowed beside it. His driveway was cleared straight down to the pavement. Smoke curled from his chimney, as he carried some extra logs that he had dug out of his buried cord inside. But today, he sat at his oak desk with metal half-glasses perched on his nose. The index finger of his left hand tapped at the lip of his teacup. The other hand ruffled the edges of a pile of manilla folders he was perusing. His back ached sorely from shoveling and pushing his snowblower, as were his arms from all the sanding. This was the day to work on his family project. It felt good to stop and rest his muscles and to kick in his brain instead.

"So, what have we here?" He asked the documents.

The place was quiet. His daughter, Kate, had hardly missed a weekend over the fall when she hadn't come up to help him. His project included cleaning and sorting. He had a lesson plan, just like he would have during his teaching days. He had set goals. 'Sometimes a principal, always a teacher,' was his motto.

Each task had a method and objectives. So far, the place was looking cared for: dusted, replaced, repaired, or cleaned. The rest discarded. Each room reflected attention. And even if it would never appear in the glossy pages of a magazine, for a newly retired educator, he felt satisfied.

"I give me an 'A' minus," he announced. "I like my old stuff polished up."

Kate had been up to the lake that week. She'd discovered some plastic tubs. In her own cleaning, she had found a plethora of small filing cabinets loaded with these manilla school folders dating back to Ed's earliest days in education. There was an entire curriculum entitled, 'Woman's History.' This had caught her attention. Years of personnel files were uncovered. Some of those included had retired back in the 1970s and 80s. Ed directed his daughter to shred most of it. But her digging had unearthed materials and information that Ed had long forgotten about. He could not even remember why he had held on to it. She placed those in question aside with a pink check. He could review them at his leisure.

After Kate left, the smell of her homemade muffins remained. She added raisins and sprinkled cinnamon on top. It was his wife Joanne's recipe. The half-eaten pastry sat beside him as he held one of the pink marked folders. Memories flooded over him at moments like this. His wife Joanne was gone six years. It was almost five 'o'clock by the time Ed sat back down before the window. He placed the folders with the pink marks on his lap, turned up the light, and wondered what Kate had found inside them that required his review.

Back in the days, before computers, the manilla folder held a wealth of paperwork in schools across America. How many of them had passed through his hands in his forty years at Alan Shepard High School? These buff-colored files were kept on everyone and everything. Secretaries spent their lives updating, refiling, and archiving them, as did most teachers and administrators. These pale, yellow folders paved the way back to all kinds of early records.

The folders before him contained information, but not grades, class standings, or awards. These looked more official in nature. They held birth dates, immigration forms, marriage and death certificates of Alan Shepard graduates. There were among them the names of soldiers killed in battles. One very yellowed form was taken from a ship's log and revealed the names of those immigrating and their completion of citizenship. Ed did notice the name Shea appeared on many. Was is just a common name, or were many related he'd often wondered?

Something happens when a person digs into old records. A window to the past opens. As a former history teacher himself, he was always interested in the past. His own family story held a special fascination for him, and he was enjoying his research into it. But it was more. The other name that appeared without fail along with the surname Shea, was MacNamara. And this was Meghan's family. How far back did the families go? Was it decades. Or more? Sally, Meghan's mother, was the family historian. Meghan seemed to be on the same track with her album project.

Ed glanced across the darkened lake. Was it his imagination, or were there more lights on at the MacNamara camp tonight? Leaning forward, Ed squinted. Then he reached for his bird watching binoculars.

"I can't believe I'm doing this," he reprimanded himself grinning.

Usually, it was the eagle or the loons he observed. There was an occasional heron also that he enjoyed following as it hunted in the early morning. But this wasn't birding.

"Well, I'll be…," he announced to no one, "Guess who's back!"

The entire camp was lit up. The roof of a red vehicle could be spotted in the driveway. His own eyes lit up. Suddenly, the season took on a whole new turn.

The files could wait.

CHAPTER 5

"A Warm Haven"

It took some jiggling to get the porch door open. It still felt odd to have to struggle with snow. Meghan had never been to the MacNamara camp during the winter. The roads had not been passable before residents began to live on the lake year-round. And between the snow wedged into the wheels of her luggage and Max's impatience to get inside, Meghan felt like a wide load on a narrow road. Her heavy coat added even more girth.

She reached up for the familiar hiding place and retrieved the key. Finally, Meghan stood before the front door and gave it a nudge. Almost bride-like, something always felt as if it carried her over the threshold. Once inside, she flicked on the ceiling light and glanced around. Her Thanksgiving tablecloth reminded her of the time-lapse since she had left. Fall leaves decorated the surface. The cornucopia sat empty, the fruits long ripened and removed. A small white index card sat perched against her wooden pepper grinder. She immediately recognized the loopy shape of the handwriting.

Welcome Meghan,

We are so sorry about not being there to greet you. As I said in my last email, Bob has a doctor's appointment in Manchester. We hope you didn't find the road too bad with all the snow.

Keep an eye out for Max. He took off just as we left. Maybe, he sensed the excitement of your return. He has been outside since around four.

The electric heat is on to keep the cold at bay. Light the fire. Bob has it set to go.

We should be back around six. So glad to have you back in time for Christmas!!!

Love Ya!

Alice & Bob

Meghan dropped the handle of her bags. She turned to Max.

"So, you have been out in the cold for about an hour. Good thing you are so furry!"

The golden retriever shook himself and then raced from room to room as if to be certain that everything was as is should be. Meghan followed in his trail turning on the lights. A sense of safety washed over her as she sensed the presence of her parents. It had always felt that way here.

With more bags to drag in, she headed back to the SUV. Her next step was to inspect the contents of the refrigerator. There must be a package of frozen hot dogs in the freezer and a leftover can of B&M baked beans on the shelves.

"Oh, Alice," she laughed, "You think of everything."

In an otherwise empty refrigerator, a white Pyrex casserole bowl sat. Lifting the lid revealed a heaping portion of what 'New Englanders' called, Chinese Pie: creamed corn, ground beef, and mashed potatoes.

Her own mother, Sally, used to make this dish. They had referred to it as 'harvest casserole.' She remembered one relative using ground lamb and calling it 'shepherd's pie.' It was the epitome of comfort food no matter what it was called. And a welcome sight on such a cold night.

Max also had dinner in his mind. He sat in front of his empty bowls and stared up at Meghan.

"Hungry?" She asked.

He wiggled his wide middle and whined.

There remained a small unopened bag of dry dog food under the sink. She filled his bowl, added water, and skimmed off some of the top layer of the hamburger from her casserole, sprinkling it on top of his food

"It's okay to spoil you sometimes," she told Max.

Setting the microwave at five minutes, Meghan placed her own dinner inside. Next to the refrigerator stood her small wine cooler. She could make out the tips of the bottles. Pulling out a single-serve Merlot, Meghan poured herself a glass. She grabbed the oblong box of long matches and headed over to the fireplace. Kindling, newspaper, and two medium-sized logs had been left. She lit the two corners; the flames quickly caught. Sipping her wine, she sat for a minute and took a deep breath.

The long flight was over. Here she sat before a warm fire. A home-cooked meal awaited her. She had fine companionship. Closing her eyes, she waited to hear the beep signal of her heated dinner.

An hour later, when Alice and Bob dropped over to check up on her, they found her just where she had sat, gingerly holding a half-full glass of Merlot, head tilted against the back of the couch, sound asleep. The fire burned brightly in the fireplace before her.

Max never made a sound. He greeted the Finches and then proceeded to curl up at Meghan's feet. Bob added two logs to the fire. Alice covered Meghan with a woolen blanket she found on the back of the couch. She removed the glass of wine from the sleeping woman's grip and set it on the kitchen table. Then they nodded to Max and quietly exited the camp, assured that their neighbor was in good hands.

For the present, all was safe and warm on Clayton shores. And everybody was finally home.

CHAPTER 6

"Glyphs"

"It's so good to have her back," Bob stated as he and his wife opened the porch door to their camp, moments later.

"She had a long day, starting in hot, arid Arizona and ending in cold, snowy New Hampshire. It will take a few days for her system to readjust."

"She must be exhausted," Alice added in agreement.

"Severe weather at both ends."

"Funny, how Max wouldn't come to us when we called him earlier. I swear, that dog has a sixth sense. Did you notice that he didn't bark when we showed up at her door like he usually does to announce an intruder?" Bob had observed.

"He will stay put for a while now that someone is at the MacNamara place," Alice noted thoughtfully.

They had stopped for a quick bite to eat on their way home, and so hadn't arrived until around six-thirty. Bob headed to the front room to watch the evening news on television. Alice headed to the kitchen.

"Aren't you coming?" Bob inquired.

"In a bit," Alice answered, "I'll put on some water for tea."

Absently, Alice hung up her coat, wrapped her scarf around the hook inside the back door, and tucked her wool and leather gloves safely inside the pockets. Heading for the stove, she retrieved the copper teapot, filled it half-way with water, and placed it on a burner, turning it to high. Her hands moved deftly but her mind was elsewhere. Her eyes looked longingly at the drawer just to the left of the refrigerator. Inside lay her abandoned Rune cards.

She had intentionally avoided her cards in weeks. She knew she needed to break her abstinence and ask for guidance. Things were back in motion and she wanted a sense of where they might go. And she was itching to get a glimpse of some hint over about Meghan's state of mind.

All her life Alice had been surrounded by soothsayers. It was in her blood. During her earlier life as a young girl, she often felt confused and lost. Someone with a touch of the mystic seemed to come along and help her. She never saw it as magic, just self-discovery. Consulting the message of the Runes meant consulting herself.

It was for this reason that she seldom used her talents unless she felt a need to help. As she lit a candle and removed the cards from the drawer, she focused on Meghan. She placed the deck before herself and set the candle behind it. She would do a short reading, just to see. She had a few minutes to herself before the water boiled.

Carefully, she shuffled the cards. Setting them before the flame of the candle, she split the deck three ways and turned over the top cards. She closed her eyes and pictured Meghan, Ed Shea, and Sam Norton. This was the situation in question. The cards that surfaced were 'Openings,' 'Unknowable,' and 'Wholeness.'

"Not much to say here," Alice sighed in disappointment.

Even the cards seemed hesitant to speak.

If Meghan had been present, Alice might have suggested an extended reading. The five-card spread was always more revealing. It offered more to think about. But this was the line she would not cross. Manipulation remained the constant danger for any guide. Fate was fate. Individuals must choose. Not the cards.

The first card, 'Openings,' reminded the reader that darkness remained in this situation. Outmoded ways needed to be reviewed and reconsidered. There was light beyond, but each person must find their own way to it.

The card stared back at Alice as if castigating her again to proceed with caution. Do not interfere. Allow Meghan to find her way it seemed to say.

The 'Unknowable' card said much the same thing. There were hidden things that had yet to be revealed. Nothing is predestined, and one must wait and see things as they occurred in their own time. Much lay ahead. Until one was actually in the future, so many things could alter the end results.

Alice was startled by the shrill whistle of her teapot. She jumped up and pulled it off the heat, pouring water into two thick pottery cups. To hers, she dropped a teabag marked 'chai.' Bob was a traditional drinker of orange pekoe. A half spoonful of honey was dripped into each from her honey dipper. She returned her gaze to the third card in Meghan's spread.

'Wholeness' was the card of self. It implied a coming into one's own as a whole person. Holy people are at peace with themselves and their choices. The light comes from within. Love always encouraged self-love, self-trust, and self-centering. Alice saw Meghan's journey coming together here on Pawtuckaway Lake. Why else would she still be here?

Often, Alice needed to remind herself that others see things differently. She so wanted what she felt was best for Meghan, but only Meghan could choose. Only Meghan could accurately translate her cards and draw meaning from them. Alice was only a medium. So, she made a note on the top sheet of her pad of paper and marked it for Meghan. Alice would share her findings and offer to do the complete five-card reading if asked. She tucked all the cards back inside their velvet bag, pulled the string tightly, and returned them to their spot, far at the back of the drawer.

Inside her head, her grandmother's words whispered-

"Do not allow your own sense of what should be, impair your

view of what is. You are not the judge of things, only another window

for others to see themselves through"

She picked up the two steaming cups of tea and decided to add some cookies. Reaching up into the top shelf of her cupboard, she removed a Blue Willow bowl that had belonged to her grandmother. It was one of the few remaining pieces to the set. She had always loved the pattern. She placed cups, a bowl of treats, and two cocktail napkins on an ornately decorated forged aluminum tray. It all came from Grandma LaFrance. Slowly, she headed in to watch the nightly news with Bob. He would wonder what took her so long.

But Bob's nose had already picked up the faint smell of burning wax that drifted into the living room. He knew that Meghan's return would drive the gypsy to emerge. He wondered what, if anything, she saw in her cards. What was the next stage in Meghan's life here on Pawtuckaway? He knew that his friend, Ed, was impacted as much as anyone by her presence. But Bob would wait. As he had learned to do.

It would all work itself out. He would choose his own moves carefully. Later.

CHAPTER 7

"Christmas Bells"

Max moaned. Meghan tried unsuccessfully to pull her cover up. It wouldn't budge. The Golden had curled himself neatly on top of the corner of the quilt. It must have held familiar scents of the camp, Jack, and the returning woman he remembered. He half-opened his eyes and glanced at the sleeping figure. She was smiling, but her eyes were closed. He nestled closer to her and they both drifted back to their dreams.

Unwilling to leave the warmth, Meghan returned to the dream she was still holding onto in her mind. In the dream, she had time-traveled back to before she was born. How many times had her mother, Sally, related the event to her? There was even a replay of it in Sally's journals. Sometime around the late 1920s, when Sally was herself a toddler, she had experienced Christmas as only one so young could. But in this dream, Meghan was an eyewitness to it.

Meghan felt the cold seeping in from under the door. She was in Sally's bedroom. Sally's own voice was speaking. Her mother smelled oatmeal. Brenda Hall would be in the kitchen at this early hour of the morning. Deep snow had fallen the night before and Dad's shovel made a scratching sound outside. He would shovel off the back porch and the walkway leading into the side door. A faint aroma of cinnamon filled the bedroom. Sally's nose wanted her to follow the seductive scent.

Sally did not want to leave her warm bed. Meghan didn't want to either. A bell rang somewhere. Was it just in her imagination? This dream felt so real. Just the way Sally had told it. Meghan could picture the home on Bell Street. There were many photos taken there over the years. She pictured the oversized dining room table when all the leaves were in. There would be an ivory linen tablecloth on it during the holidays. A bowl full of fruit would sit in the center. Wrapped around the banister leading downstairs would be a green garland. Sally had told her story so many times and with such detail, it was as if Meghan herself trailed her mother from her bedroom, down to the warm bowl of oatmeal.

Again, a bell rang. Sally wore her robe and knitted slippers down the stairs; she could almost taste the cinnamon in the warm cereal.

Suddenly, an image of a sled speeding down the familiar hill of Derryfield came into view. Faster and faster it went. Sally had taken Meghan there during winters many times. Santa came on such a vehicle, only much bigger to handle all the toys. And his sleigh went way faster than any other sled. Meghan could smell the cold air as the sled sped along. Then, Sally opened the door to the front hall. It was cold and she hurried to the door leading to the back of the house. Just beyond the dining room, she could already feel warm air reach her face. Glancing to the side of the dining room were two windows. She heard some stomping and looked out, expecting to see her father just brushing himself off to come in and eat breakfast. But it wasn't her father there on the porch.

Sally recalled that her eyes were still crusted with sleep. She rubbed them and stopped to get a better look at the strange figure on their back porch. The man had a long white beard. His eyes were blue, and they peered in at her from under a red stocking hat. A gloved hand pushed the hat back on his head only to reveal a head full of white hair. The hair was long and fell to his shoulders. He was dressed all in red. She redirected herself toward the side of the dining room and toward the window. In a blink of an eye, the man had disappeared.

Sally had told her childhood tale so many times. But in this dream, Meghan watched as her mother screamed and ran to the kitchen.

"Santa. Santa Claus. I saw him! He was on the porch!"

Brenda Hall, Sally's mother, was said to have turned from stirring the hot pot of oatmeal, bent down, and with tears in her eyes kissed Sally. Her father stood in the doorway and had smiled and nodded.

Meghan opened her eyes. She was disoriented for a split second. Her own eyes were filled with tears. She remembered where she was. Max stirred.

"Oh, Max," she said softly, "Just a dream."

But such an occurrence imprints itself deeply in a child's imagination and on those who hear the event retold many times. A million Christmas moments would be experienced by the Hall family, the MacNamara family, and families across America. Meghan put the date to be around 1928, from the journal entries she had from that year. Sally clearly never forgot it. Few Christmases would be like the ones before 1929. A lot of magic went out of it for so many others.

Now, wide awake, Meghan heard a bell ringing. Max jumped up from the comfort of his spot and began to bark. She recognized it as coming from her cell phone, but couldn't even guess which bag it had been buried in.

Slowly, she was back. It was December 2014. Memories of Bell street were a long way from the winter on Pawtuckaway Lake. The dream of Sally's childhood Christmas morning evaporated in the light of day.

CHAPTER 8

***

"Catching Up"

"Now, Alice," Bob began, "Let the woman settle in. I am quite aware of your late-night voodoo," he added teasingly.

Alice shrugged. She sat knitting another scarf beside the fireplace. Her jaw tightened. She hadn't touched her Rune cards in weeks. Her productivity of handmade scarves had increased as a result. And when she had finally given in to the impulse, she found little guidance there. She really had nothing to report to her neighbor.

"I just wanted to invite her over for some of my homemade turkey soup," Alice retorted sounding more defensive than she had intended.

"I called her and left an invite to come over for lunch. She hasn't returned my call. Max arrived about an hour ago," she said and pointed to the red scarf around the dog's neck.

Bob rolled his eyes and chuckled at the sight of the dog's festive appearance.

"Max seems quite happy that she is back. Poor fella has already lost one owner." Bob spoke these words more to the dog than to his wife. He rubbed Max's head as he spoke, absently straightening the Golden's red accessory.

As if on command, there was a quick rap on the door. Max headed straight it. Bob could see Meghan's familiar profile through the door's windowpane.

"My phone is low on juice. In my travels it ran down. So, I couldn't reply to your offer. Are you still serving lunch?" She inquired.

For a split second, Alice thought that her neighbor looked different. So much like Sally with her hair tucked up under a winter hat. Meghan looked fuller in her winter clothes, more rested, and happier. Alice hoped that Meghan's time away had helped her settle much that remained unsettled here.

"I'll leave you two to catch up," Bob quickly offered.

He gave Meghan a warm hug and picked up his buffalo plaid woolen shirt. He planned on going to the shed and working on the seats of his boat. He lifted his portable space heater up for inspection.

"It's cold in there this time of year," he said as he headed out.

Alice offered Meghan two empty hooks near the door for her coat. She pulled a pair of woolen socks out from under a bench beneath the hooks.

"Wear these. The wooden floors are cold. I need to dig out my scatter rugs."

Max headed for a corner in the kitchen where a woolen blanket had been placed for him. He turned in circles until he had it just right, then he leaned his hind quarter against the wall and placed the rest of himself to face the ladies. It appeared that all was well in his world.

Alice began to pull out utensils from the drawer to the right of the sink. She found two large mugs in her oaken cabinet and retrieved a ladle from a pottery jar. Using both arms, she withdrew a large pot of cold soup from the refrigerator. From it, she filled the mugs to the brim and popped them in the microwave. Next, she laid a long stick of artisan French bread on a wooden cutting and lifted the top off a fresh block of creamy Irish butter.

"Want some hot cider?" Alice inquired.

The smell of hot cinnamon in the mulled cider caught Meghan by surprise because of her vivid dream the night before. She stopped for a moment before answering.

"I'd love some. The cinnamon smells incredible."

Meghan had placed the clean empty casserole dish on the counter when she arrived.

"Straight away, I need to go to the market," she began, "Your Chinese Pie last night was so delicious. Thanks, so much."

Alice nodded and continued to lay out their lunch.

"Let's see. Since you were gone, a few things did happen. The Campbells had their babies. Twins." Alice suddenly blurted out. "They are Alec and Ariel."

"I wondered when she was due back in June when she was already showing. How is she?"

"She is doing fine. There was a baby shower for her and of course she got doubles of everything."

"I'll need to buy her something. Diapers are always a good start."

"Corky stayed with us for a few days while Judy was in the hospital. She and Max had a great time together playing in the snow. Max shared his blanket with her."

Alice said, nodding toward the corner where Max opened his eyes at the sound of his name.

The microwave beeped and Alice placed two steaming cups of turkey soup on the table. She cut the bread stick into thick slices and slid the softened butter in Meghan's direction.

"How did it go in Arizona?" Alice continued.

"Lots of damage at first. So much wind and rain. We were very lucky to have some federal help. I feel like a storm chaser. One end there is warm and severe weather, while here it was cold and snowy."

"We sure had the snow and ice. I can't tell you how good it was to get electricity back on. And we were lucky to get it back so soon."

Alice said as she absently wiped a piece of breadcrumb from the table with her finger.

Looking out onto the white lake surface, gray clouds floating above a line of black treetops, Meghan commented dreamily.

"But it is so pretty. Isn't it?"

Alice caught a faraway expression pass over Meghan's face as the women sipped their soup.

"You were so fast to put up your little tree!" Alice commented. "It looked so festive there on the deck when Bob and I pulled in last night."

A puzzled look crossed Meghan's face.

"I thought you and Bob put it there," Meghan replied.

"No."

"I wonder who did."

An awkward silence followed. Metal hit glass as spoons dipped into warm soup. Neither woman spoke for what seemed an eternity. Both women focused on their lunches. Alice got up to get Meghan a Christmas-themed paper napkin. They each had come to different conclusions: Alice hoped it was Ed Shea. Meghan guessed it was Sam Norton. Neither vocalized their thoughts.

Meghan had returned but all that was unresolved remained so. She was the first to speak.

"So, how did Thanksgiving go?"

Alice put all thoughts of Ed and Sam aside. Her attempts to find answers for Meghan in the cards had proven futile. She did wish for just one second, however, that she had offered Meghan a glass of wine instead of hot cider.

The women related their Thanksgiving holidays. Alice rated the Pie Walk as a total success. She let Meghan know that the Class of 1974 Reunion had never materialized but might take place during the summer, over at the Pawtuckaway campgrounds. The students looked forward to a warmer date. Meghan admitted to having a wonderful turkey dinner with her Arizona neighbors, about the departure of her first tenants, and the arrival of new ones. She also detailed the multiple repairs that had been done on her western home.

"My new tenants are an older couple and they think that I must really like snow to return here."

The women chatted as they cleared the table and filled the dishwasher. Then it was Alice's turn to initiate conversation.

"Are your family members planning to return here for Christmas?" Alice began.

"I hope so. I felt so badly about the Thanksgiving bust."

"Hampton Hills has a lot of activities planned for the Christmas season. I will leave you a copy of the schedule. There is the craft fair, the dance, and the tree lighting. There is talk of snow sculptures with all this snow!"

As they headed for the door, Meghan turned toward her hostess and paused.

"I had a lot of time to think while I was away. I do need to resolve my heart. I really think that I will come to some resolution while I am here. Christmas has always been my favorite time of year."

Alice knew she had an opening. As she helped Meghan with the door and watched her wrap her scarf around her neck, she decided to make her move.

"I'd be glad to do a spread for you, if you like."

Meghan smiled.

"I need to finish my family album. Their story is easier to tell, sometimes. But, yes, I will take you up on that offer. Thanks, for everything," Meghan added.

Alice watched as Meghan trudged through the snow between their houses, Max at her heals.

"Christmas is all about family– and love. I hope they both find you this year." Alice said to the pair as they passed the twinkling tree and disappeared inside.

And for one quick second, an image of Meghan's father, Jack, crossed her mind. He and Max had followed the same path from the Finch's many times before. Alice felt a tug at her heart for Jack's daughter and his faithful dog.

CHAPTER 9

"Digging into Christmas"

Christmas was on the horizon, yet the camp remained stuck in Thanksgiving, with napkins, tablecloth, and plates reflecting the colors of fall. Scooping up orange pumpkins and gourds, Meghan eyed her empty cornucopia and sighed. She needed to replace them with the colors of the season. She had little here and planned to get to the local dollar store to pick up something festive to redecorate it with. She was going into Hampton Hills with the Finch's to drop off the rental and would take the opportunity to shop.

As she collected up her autumn decor, she remembered that there was a box marked Christmas out in the shed. There must be something there she could at least re-purpose. Even a string of lights would be useful. Her parents always strung them on the railings of the porch. It was worth a "look see" as Jack would say, "before going out to buy more."

She glanced at herself in the bathroom mirror and wondered about her own appearance. She remembered to pack some of her warmer clothes from Arizona when she returned. Her hair had really gotten long while she was away. Something special to wear for Christmas was clearly another thing to consider.

Max sat patiently by the front door. He had hardly left her side since she had arrived.

"Let's see if we have some Christmas stored in the shed," she offered with excitement.

It would take some clearing to reach the outbuilding. She only had the small garden shovel perched in the sand bucket. She made another mental note to purchase a decent one at the first opportunity she got. This would have to do for now.

Slowly, Meghan dug a narrow path. It was silly to be doing this, but once Meghan got an idea in her head, she followed through. Sally had said as much so many times.

"Just like your father." Sally's voice echoed against the silent winter scene.

Almost half an hour later, Meghan had reached the front door of the wooden structure. Setting her tiny tool against the outside wall, she attempted to pull open the door. Again, she lifted more snow away with her hands. Max rolled on his back in the path she had created. Suddenly, he bolted after a gray squirrel that ran past. Meghan had worked up a sweat, but she was almost there. She pulled the door back enough to step inside.

From the doorway, she spotted the brown box on top of the cupboard. Back in July, she had noted it, but had put off sorting it. She pulled over Jack's red wooden step ladder, spread the legs, and flattened the treads. Wondering all along if it would hold her. It did. She reached far back and pushed the box forward so that she could lift it down. It was light.

Once back on level ground, Meghan unfolded the top. She wondered whose hands had folded the four lids into the familiar interlocking design. She pulled them apart. Sure enough, the box held a string of old colored lights. They were the large coated bulbs used in her childhood. She pulled them out and lay them on the floor beside the box. Smaller boxes held glass bulbs and a mixture of ornaments. Many were familiar, others reflected souvenirs her parents had collected on trips. A white 'Celtic Cross' had been carefully wrapped in tissue paper, a wooden snowman proved to be in remarkably good condition, and then there were the porcelain and brass pieces that held miniature portraits of her and her brother, Kevin. A porcelain Golden Retriever looked up from a bed of paper napkins, coincidentally wearing a red scarf not unlike the one on Max.

"Max, Jack even had you on his tree," Meghan heard herself say.

Max had wiggled himself in and was busy sniffing under Jack's workbench. Meghan suspected that mice had found a cozy home for the winter there, using the opening Max had found in the corner of the shed weeks before. It seemed ages since Pete, Ed's handyman, had come by to do some work for her. He'd never gotten to the task of covering this hole in the floor.

Further searching inside the cardboard box revealed a pack of caroling songbooks, their elastic band disintegrated. The bottom of the box was lined with old Christmas cards; Meghan recognized many of the signatures. She discovered a metal container marked 'Sucrets.' Jack MacNamara never discarded the old lozenges tins after he had finished with the contents. Inside were extra hooks on which to hang ornaments. An unopened package of tinsel sat waiting underneath it all.

She clearly had a fine start on Christmas. This would solve much of her tree dilemma. Leaning against the far wall was the old tree stand. An inside tree was beginning to take shape. She needed more to fill in a tree but would employ her family to contribute the rest. And handmade items would give her tree the character she was looking to create

As Meghan made her way back to the camp, carrying her treasure trove. The tiny tree lights winked from the mystery tree on her deck. She still didn't know who was responsible for the gift. Her eyes drifted over to something green buried in the snow; she remembered that her kayak was now quite buried. Sun had exposed the very top of the bow. Instinctively, Meghan's eyes shifted to the lake and in the direction of Ed Shea's camp. She sighed. Who was it that she really wanted to have left her this evergreen?

Once on the porch, Meghan stomped her boots, wiped off Max's back, and headed inside. She replaced her miniature shovel back inside the sand pail Bob had provided her with. He seldom used any salt feeling that salt was too strong so near to the lake water She felt the warmth as she wiggled out of her scarf, hat, and gloves, and pushed her coat up onto the wall hook. The light on her answering machine blinked red. She pressed play.

"Hi, Mom. Welcome back. Call me. Is there enough snow, heat, and food?"

It was her son Kevin.

"Hi. It's Ann. Out already? Stay warm. I'll call you later when I'm out of school."

Then there was a click. Someone had hung up. Jack's old machine no longer logged in the identity of the caller, so Meghan had no way of knowing who it had been. Maybe, Bob, to remind her about their drive into town. Maybe someone else.

"Here we go again," Meghan moaned to herself.

She headed into the kitchen and found a jar of peanut butter. She had thawed a loaf of bread and would eat it for lunch. Tea was plentiful in her camp. Clearly, shopping was her number one priority.

"I owe Alice. Big time!"

She pulled the magnetic shopping list from the side of the refrigerator and had to laugh. The pad depicted two beach chairs set before a calm, sunny lake. Christmas was less than two weeks off. Time had gotten away from her. There was so much to do and so little time to do it in.

Alice had said that they were heading into town around one. It was already after one. He had bandages to be removed from his hand. Apparently, Bob had gotten quite a gash while working on his boat. Between the car accident and this, Alice was beating a path to the doctor's office lately. Many others were slipping on ice and spraining wrists, she had confided. Bob didn't let a little blood stop him.

Meghan was to drop off her rental and meet them later. They would go to the market together and return in the Finch's car. Her own red truck still needed snow tires. That was another thing to add to her lengthening list.

She changed into better clothes and stuffed her 'to-do' list inside her backpack. She gobbled down the remainder of her peanut butter sandwich and poured the rest of her tea into the sink. Just as she pulled on her coat, a car horn sounded. The Finches were here.

"Stay," she ordered Max.

He had water. Alice said that he was used to being left alone for a few hours and would be fine. Sometimes, he snuck up on the couch to nap, but other than that, he would not try to get out.

He whined softly as she closed the door behind.

CHAPTER 10

"Slippery Paths"

"It's a Christmas village." Meghan pronounced the words as she pulled her rental car into the Campbell's Auto Repair parking lot. The Finch's waved and beeped as they continued on to their appointment.

"Hampton Hills in snow. How beautiful!" Meghan told Sam Campbell.

Snow still covered the church roof. The abandoned train station seemed prepared to greet passengers arriving for the season. An oversized wreath hung jauntily from its old roof. The rusty red structure, with its forest green trim, looked picture perfect. For a moment, Meghan could almost picture a steaming engine along with the passenger cars and trailing caboose. It was the season for homecomings.

Snowbanks lined the road making it narrow; tree limbs hung down creating a tunnel effect. Houses along the route sunk deeply in white, green garland wrapped like gift ribbons along their doorways and porch rails. A wooden manger nestled in front of the church. Sam had erected a larger-than-life Santa next to his business sign. The sign shone multi-color with the letters C-A -M-P-B-E-L-L outlined in white lights.

Suddenly Sam stood outside her car window.

"Hello. Nice to see you," he said before she could speak.

"Hello, yourself. Twins! How wonderful is that?" Meghan blurted back.

Sam's eyes sparked with pride, but deep circles underneath revealed sleepless nights.

"How is everybody?" Meghan continued as she stepped out of the rental.

"Great. Just tired."

"Thanks, for this."

"No problem. I know the rental guy at the airport. I do work for them. He comes by on Saturday."

"You have a ride back?" Sam inquired as he took her keys.

"All set."

"Got to go. Cars really take a beating in this weather. Good for business though," he said with a wry smile. "I'll send you the forms. Have you got email?"

"Yes."

Meghan decided to take up snow tires another time. Sam had his hands full. So, she strapped on her backpack and headed on toward the market.

One must live in New Hampshire to realize just how unique the four seasons are here. Visiting a summer resort in mid- December, it is hard to imagine that the state can experience such contrasting weather. Winter in New England holds unfathomable beauty when it is ninety degrees only months later. The cold, ice, and dark is as much a part of New England as the hot, humid, and light. But once winter arrives, there is little as spectacular as the "Currier and Ives" scenes that follow a significant snowfall. Hampton Hills reflected such seasonal imagery. Meghan's eyes took in the colorful decorations the residents had added. Summer heat felt as far away as Arizona at that moment.

Annette's hair shop came up on the right. Impulsively, Meghan decided to pop in and see if she could make an appointment. It was one thing to shove her hair inside a hat, but another to comb it into submission. She glanced absently at the parking lot but didn't recognize any of the cars. She pulled in and headed for the entrance. The bells attached to the top of the door rang brightly as Meghan stepped inside. Two unfamiliar women sat in the chairs; one drying under the air, the other being worked on. Annette looked up at the sound of the bells and waved with her head. Her eyes shot a glance toward the woman under the hairdryer. It took Meghan a second to catch on. The client's face was hidden behind a magazine.

Annette rolled the last curler and excusing herself approached the reception desk.

"Welcome back, hon," Annette greeted Meghan.

"Any chance of an opening. I so need a cut," Meghan replied.

Alice investigated the book of appointments on the desk. She slowly picked up a card and studied the calendar. With little movement, she handed Meghan a card with a date and time. Meghan noticed how robotic she was behaving and wished she had called instead of showing up. But Annette winked as she handed the card to her.

"Saturday. At one. See you then." Annette said turning abruptly back to her awaiting customers.

Meghan quickly left. She felt as if she had been presumptuous to drop by; Alice was acting oddly. She checked the time and day on her card before stuffing it inside her backpack. Annette had scrawled a note on the top. It read- 'Sam is back in town.'

Meghan took a closer look at the vehicles in Annette's lot. One car had the vanity plate 'CELLIT' on it. Had it been Suzy under the hairdryer? Meghan felt her hands grip the card Annette had just given her, another reason to wonder if Sam had been by her place. And how did she feel about that?

She felt a cold chill. Her left foot slipped from under her. Catching herself before she fell, Meghan breathed in. She choked on the sudden coldness hitting her lungs. What did it all mean? And when would she know for sure. She directed herself toward the market. Provisions were her priority. Her hair could wait. Or could it?

CHAPTER 11

"Broken Limbs"

Alice sat for a moment in the reception area of the doctor's office. Meghan should be arriving any minute. Two other patients sat opposite to them, reading "Newsweek" and "People" magazine. They paid little notice to the couple. Bob said nothing as he fiddled with the new support the doctor had suggested he wear until hit wrist was stronger. Alice watched, already anticipating his resistance to such a contraption.

The door swung open and Meghan stepped inside. Cold air swept through the room and the nurse looked up from the phone with an inquisitive look. She quickly nodded at the Finches.

Alice smiled a little too brightly. Meghan wondered how serious Bob's injuries were. Did we all fake it as we aged, not wanting to accept the unalterable effects of aging? No one spoke for a moment. Bob and Alice rose and began to zip up their jackets and to pull on woolen mittens. Meghan recognized they both wore handiwork from Alice around their necks. She looked forward to a nice wool scarf from them for Christmas.

"I forget how quickly it gets dark now," Meghan offered, "But the lights are so festive all over town !"

Again, there was an awkward silence as the three left the office. Meghan had left her backpack and brown bag of groceries on the porch outside. She slipped on the straps and used both arms to lift her purchases. All plans to pick up more Christmas items had gone as thoughts of Sam Norton filled her head.

"Did you bump into anyone you know?" Alice asked as they opened the door of the Finch's SUV. Alice took the driver's seat. Bob seldom did not drive and struggled with the seat belt. Meghan dropped her items in the backseat and settled herself in.

Alice waited for a response.

"Yes, I did," She began, "I chatted with the sister of a former student at the market. She had planned to fly in from New York for the reunion. I need to look her up. I can't remember an Ellie. But she may have only been in Mr. Norton's class."

Meghan was glad she was sitting in the back seat as she said Sam's name. Alice appeared to be too focused on her driving to notice anything.

But Alice drove her passengers and cargo back Rt 156 and on toward the lake saying nothing. She turned onto Mountain Road seemingly lost in her own thoughts.

"How 's your hand?" Meghan finally asked remembering her manners.

"It's fine," Bob quickly replied.

"He needs to use a brace for a while. He did get a minor sprain. The cut needed two stitches, though, so he should keep it dry for a few days," Alice pronounced with authority.

Bob sighed softly.

But Meghan's thoughts returned to the note on her appointment card. She regarded her reflection in the rear-view mirror and wondered at herself. Tiny gray hairs seemed to have sprung up around her hairline. Should she have Annette color it? Her green eyes might need more mascara. Could her cheeks use more color? Was she just overheating from the heater in the vehicle? Or was it more than that? And what about those festive clothes? Perhaps, a new dress or woolen sweater would look better than her father's barn jacket and down vest. Why did it suddenly matter how she looked, anyway?

Alice began chatting as they made their way down toward Clayton Circle, pointing out tricky turns in the road and reminding Meghan about tires. Bob too piped up and suggested she have Sam Campbell see if her tires were fit for all seasons. Meghan half listened.

Then the Finch's exchanged some discussion about what they would have for dinner. Should Alice thaw out some ham and make omelets? They could have it with raisin toast. She had some nice cinnamon tea. Wasn't there a special on PBS to watch later?

Carefully, Alice turned the vehicle around the last corner and down the small slope toward both camps. Automatically, Meghan looked to see her mother's birdhouse. Black branches seemed frail and thin under the thick coating of snow. She strained to find the familiar copper roof. But as they reached the last of the hills and turned into her driveway, Meghan was still unable to locate the landmark sight. In fact, she thought she saw a long branch half buried at the foot of the tree where the tiny house had hung for years. An ache started in her stomach and grew.

"You can just drop me here," Meghan managed to mutter.

Alice and Bob looked across and out of the passenger door as their neighbor seemed to be in a hurry to escape the confines of their SUV. Had they chatted too much? Did the woman need some space? Alice had offered her an omelet too, but she hadn't replied. What seemed to have upset her? They thought they knew but would not inquire further.

Meghan's head bobbed along behind the snow piles. She looked so young with her backpack and bangs sticking out around her forehead. They pulled out and Alice tapped the horn. The door to the MacNamara camp opened and Meghan waved back, disappearing inside. The Finch's looked at one another and took a dramatic breath simultaneously.

"Do you think she saw him?" Alice blurted out.

"She didn't say so. But he had just left the doctor's office minutes before she arrived."

"She seemed anxious to get home."

"Maybe, it was something else bugging her."

They stopped the engine and Alice watched as Bob used his good arm to open the passenger door. Ed Shea too had seemed to be in no mood to chat. He came for his annual flu shot and left the doctor's office with barely a word to them. Was she just making too much of it all?

"Here we go again," Bob muttered under his breath.

An hour later, Alice watched as Meghan and Max walked down to the frozen shoreline of the lake. She continued to watch them walk toward the dock. Alice noticed that the pair turned and stared back at the camp where a twinkling evergreen silently announced itself.

Meghan's eyes looked at the same scene, from the dock, where she and Max now stood. Max sat down and waited. Meghan turned toward the lake and then turned to face the camp.

Alice wondered what she saw.

Meghan looked beyond the tiny tree and back into the deep snowy woods where her mother's birdhouse should have been. She stopped and stared until the cold began to penetrate her feet.

"Come on, Max," she said.

"Moods change like the clouds," Sally's voice advised.

Things had changed. And Meghan had to catch up. Soon.

1929

Entry from the Past

Dear Diary,

It's Christmas and the boys will find this holiday somewhat simpler than usual. News is bleak. Jobs are ending. We are uncertain about the economy. Wil owned a lot of stock. The Model T needs some work, but it sits in the garage. Mike had hoped to buy his own car. But that looks unlikely.

Each son will get something new, but only one thing each. Little Jack wanted a bicycle. Not this year. Ted's old one will have to do.

Ted wanted a new suit of clothes to wear to a dance. He'll have to borrow one of Wil's. Maybe, I can alter a jacket from Mike's old ones. Luckily, I can shorten and fold up cuffs. Lately, the boys have become used to making do.

I've never seen so much pessimism in the papers. None of our friends are holding any sort of holiday party. Constant worry and fear taint most conversations.

I hope 1930 will be a good year.

— Agnes MacNamara

CHAPTER 12

"Christmas Past"

Her American chop suey casseroles were finished. Meghan's first job was to make two of them and bring one over to the Finch's. Perfect comfort fare, she decided. The recipe was simple- ground beef, canned tomatoes, onions, elbow macaroni, and some spices. Her own refrigerator was finally filling up with vegetables, fruits, and juices. It was all she could carry on her first visit to the market.

Why was it that cold weather demanded these hearty dishes? And after the warmth of Arizona, Meghan really craved her carbohydrates. Still, she couldn't seem to keep her feet warm. Jack had a drawer full of thick socks he must have worn while ice fishing. They were getting much used these days.

The entry in Agnes's diary lay open on the kitchen table. The words ran through her mind as she looked around the camp and tried to picture her own Christmas plans.

"Max, I need to decorate."

Max had already poked his curious nose into the boxes she had pulled from the shed. The string of lights lay on the floor, plugged into a wall outlet. Miraculously all but four worked.

The carefully wrapped wooden snowman lay on top of the couch, still in tissue. Four miniature brass French horns would need a little polishing but would look great on their tree. Meghan had gotten sidetracked with the collection of yellowed Christmas cards, finding even more recent ones that Jack must have received from friends here on the lake. She might string them as she had seen done. Her assortment of past decorations was adding up. The camp was not that large, but she really needed now was a nice shapely tree.

Meghan walked over to her grandmother's open diary and re-read the entry. Eighty-five years had passed since jack's own mother faced down the task of recreating a special holiday for her family. Did little Jack wander down that morning and find no bike? Did Ted feel inadequate in the old suit he'd had to borrow for his special dance? When did Wil realize that he had to leave Manchester, New Hampshire, to find work? So much sat on the verge that Christmas past. And here she was recalling them all and undertaking a similar job. With so much more to do with. Agnes looked ahead with hope, not knowing that it was just that hope that would carry American families forward.

Loss is an intricate part of holidays. It remains the responsibility of a mother's creativity to make a warm place for a family. It was alright to remember, but not to dwell in the past. It was about gathering together and being thankful which made holidays memorable. Agnes' words reached across decades to be read here by the daughter of her youngest son. Meghan didn't know Agnes, and yet she did.

As Meghan lifted and placed her findings on windowsills and tabletops, she could feel the hands of those who had used them before her. Suddenly, she pulled down the folding ladder and climbed up into the small room in the rafters and sat before the window. She tossed the red plaid pillows down to the room below. She would add them to the brown ones already on the couch.

It was unusual for her to be up where all the boys insisted on sleeping. She could barely stand erect. The blue spines of Jack's collection of Hardy Boys mysteries reminded her that three generations of men had come up here. She sat down and took in the wide view of Pawtuckaway, feeling like a bird in a tree.

"Christmas on the lake," she whispered.

Max whined at the bottom of the ladder.

She heard the sound of her phone. She could not reach it from here, so she sat and tried to listen. The caller didn't leave any message.

"Someone is trying to reach us," she said to Max as she descended the ladder and pushed it back up into its ceiling frame.

And she needed to contact the outside world as well.

When she was ready.

CHAPTER 13

"Reconnecting"

Despite frozen roads, dented cars, buried porches, and snow melting and refreez-ing, the lakers of Pawtuckaway seemed undaunted. Meghan headed over to the Finch's with a still-warm American chop suey casserole in her arms. Max led the way. Fortunately, Bob had already cleared a path.

"Well, good morning," Bob hollered over from the deck where he was pull-ing out a single log from his stash.

"Thanks, for clearing a path between our houses. First on my list is to invest in a winter shovel," Meghan responded. " No more shoveling. Not with that arm." She added with firmness.

She stomped her boots of the snow and followed Bob inside.

"Well, old boy. Nice to see you," He crooned as he rubbed the dogs ample behind.

Max stood, nose in the air, enjoying the attention.

"Alice is off already. She had an appointment for a haircut and then said she would be at the library. She volunteers there over the winter."

She handed him the glass-covered Pyrex dish. He sniffed the air and smiled.

"Want coffee?" He offered.

"No, thanks. But I need to use your computer to send off some emails. My computer is not working, yet. Do you mind?"

"Not at all. You are not alone. I hear that an entire cell tower was toppled by the snow and wind. We are on the outer circle of civilization," He joked, "and we love it."

Bob led Meghan down the hall to the small room where they kept their computer. As they passed the dining room table, she could smell cinnamon. Like toy soldiers, a lineup of small loaves sat wrapped in aluminum foil. A roll of red ribbon awaited the final touch. They were most likely going to the church fair.

He logged on and left her alone. "I'll let you to it."

Max followed him back to the front of the house. Meghan opened her coat and hung it on the back of the chair. She pulled off her scarf and mittens and stuffed them inside the sleeve. She wiggled her fingers of cold before she began. There were no messages from Sam.

Meghan blamed the absence of her own computer for that. He may have tried to reach her. She had been missing messages since she arrived. But why not leave her one on the phone?

Sam had a new email address. She had used it while in Arizona. She typed in: biglakeSam.com.

Hello,

Arrived safely. So much snow! Roads here are passable.

Looking forward to Christmas. What are your plans? Glad to be back.

She sat back and re-read it. Was it too casual? Should she have said more? As an afterthought she added—

Don't have email yet.

That was enough for now she thought. And signed it simply:

Meghan.

She read it all again and then hit Send. The other emails were so much easier. She sent them to Kevin, her brother in England, and to her two children, Ann and Ted.

Hello All,

Plan to hold Christmas at the lake. Want you all to come.

Call me. I am using my neighbor's computer.

Miss you all!

—Love, Mom.

She had kept in touch with her family while in Arizona. But not until she arrived did she really think that she might hold the holiday on the lake. If she could get there, so could they, she'd thought. Now it was official. She would plan accordingly. And use some of Agnes' special ingredient - hope.

She stood up and headed back toward the front of the Finch's camp, feeling as if her plans were falling into place. Bob's back faced her. He was working on something at the counter. She could see the white of the bandages on his hand. He turned and Max rose groggily from his nap beside the door.

"All set?"

"Yes. I just needed everyone to know that I am settled in."

Meghan began to snap the front of her coat and pull on her mittens.

"So, will the family be in for Christmas?"

Bob casually inquired as he pat Max's head.

"That's the plan. With so much snow, it feels like Christmas already."

"No question about a white Christmas this year," Bob chuckled.

"I'm off to the hardware store to buy a shovel, some garland, replacement bulbs and hopefully, a wreath."

"What about your tires?"

"Oh, Sam says that I have all weather tires," Meghan responded.

Before heading out, Meghan turned and decided to ask the question she had been wanting to ask.

"Any idea who left the lighted tree?"

Bob looked over at it and made a face. He looked back at the woman before him and seemed to stall.

"Well, whoever it was, Max didn't bark. We would have heard him. Few people get within fifty feet of your place or ours without him announcing their arrival."

Typical response, Meghan thought.

"We are so glad you are back. We hope you really do settle things here during this trip," Bob added.

He picked up a red flyer and handed it to her.

"The schedule of holiday events here in town. Hope you go. We are a community that enjoys this season."

Bob seemed to lock his lips sometimes, as if demonstrating his firmness to say no more.

Max remained behind, apparently confident that his mistress was back for good. Or perhaps anticipating some taste of the smells he had been taking in from the dining room table.

"I love Christmas. And I do feel at home here," Meghan assured him.

Looking over the long list of events, she commented that it looked very inviting. She would plan on coming to some.

"Be good," she instructed Max.

Someone had left her this tiny present on her deck. And that someone was a familiar person.

Was that someone Ed?

CHAPTER 14

"A Cut to the Truth"

Downtown Hampton Hills never looked as lovely as it did that day; snowbanks reached halfway up most street signs and posts, windows peered through crystal coats of ice, roofs dipped deeply into green bushes. With only a string of lights the town had become a winter wonderland. Evergreen trees outlined the main road as if awaiting a holiday parade to pass through. Wreaths hung from many front doors. Warm lights reflected golden from porches on the sparkly sidewalks. Alice only had to take it all in as she steered her vehicle toward the beauty shop.

A quick glance at herself in the rear-view mirror was a rude reminder of just how much time had elapsed since her last appointment. Everything was dressed for the holidays except her.

Even from the road, Alice could see Annette's decorations. A life-sized snowman perched on the veranda guarded the entrance. The front door looked like a giant gift, wrapped in green and red sparkly paper and tied with a plaid bow. The sign outside with the cursive name, 'Annette,' had been outlined in colored lights. On the front lawn of snow, an automated deer dipped and raised its head as if grazing; silver sparkles danced on its back as it moved. The final touches of balsam green garland wound itself around the banister and the porch railing. Alice could faintly hear music coming from inside. She parked, stepped out of her car, and looked back over her shoulder to take it all in.

Making her way to the sanded walkway and up the front steps, she pulled the front door open and noticed a black sleigh full of wrapped gifts sitting just beyond the lot. It was obvious why these displays had won ribbons many times in the past. Annette had outdone herself again.

More music met Alice's ears as she stepped inside. Annette wore a set of those bobbly antlers on her head; the bells tinkled as the hairdresser moved around a small client. She clipped and fussed at the girl's bangs but quickly motioned for Alice to come inside.

"Hello. Have a seat," Annette invited.

Inside was equally a vision of the season. Annette's collections of Santas lined the railing that ran along the edge of the ceiling. An oversized white poinsettia crowded the main counter. White and pale green lights lined an unused mantelpiece. Nestled in the center sat the old manger set that had been hand carved by Annette's grandfather in Canada. More bells rang above the door. Looking up, Alice noticed four wooden letters arranged jauntily on top of the door frame. They read 'NOEL.'

Annette chatted brightly with the small girl and her grandmother. Effortlessly, Annette would spill into French with the older women and then back into English with the youngster. Alice forgot sometimes that Annette could speak both so fluently. She tried to understand some of the words. She had heard it as a girl, but rarely after that. There remained a strong French-Canadian tie in New Hampshire still. And in the smaller towns you often heard the older population use it among themselves.

Annette was finishing up and brushed off the child's shoulders. The cape also reflected the season and was sprinkled with red elves and snowflakes against a green background. Still chattering in and out of French and English, she offered the child and her grandmother a candy cane, accepted her payment, and wished then them all a *Joyeux Noel*. Alice recognized the girl say, *'un sucre d'orge,'* and smiled. She remembered the French way of saying the tasty, striped treat.

Alice automatically headed for the other empty chair as the two left. Quickly, Annette swept the floor clean and draped a large cape with the same holiday pattern over Alice.

Alice wondered if hairdressers did these motions in their sleep.

"Boy, your hair is really long!" Annette announced as she pulled a clean comb through it.

She quickly directed Alice toward the sink where, gently, she lay Alice's head on the edge and turned on the faucets. Expertly, laying her arm on the edge, Annette tested the temperature, nodded in Alice's direction, and squirted some shampoo onto her own hands. Alice laid back. This was Alice's favorite part.

Even though Annette's movements were efficient, her hands were gentle. A thing of beauty some said. So, Alice's shoulders dropped, her breath slowed, and her eyes closed. For the next few minutes, there was nothing between her scalp but fingers. Every corner of her head would be messaged. Not since childhood had anyone done such a shampoo. Alice had some experience with meditation and compared this to it. Christmas music played softly in the background as suds swarmed all over Alice's head; all became as white as snow in her mind. She could sit here all day; she had often felt she might fall asleep.

As Alice melted in the chair, Annette hummed and even whistled softly. She chatted off and on, but the words were mostly lost in the movement of her hands over Alice's scalp. Until something Annette had just said penetrated Alice's trance.

"Sam Norton."

Alice had heard it. She was shaken aback. Opening her eyes, she suddenly tuned in.

"My sister was up in Wolfeboro doing Christmas shopping last week. She thinks she saw what she described as that good-looking realtor. When she was up last summer, she remembered the couple. He would have been still engaged to Suzy Timberly then. I told her how he had moved up to the big lake,

Winnipesaukee– and those huge commissions. They say that Suzy does alright here on Pawtuckaway Lake, what with her family owing the agency. Then my sister said that she thought that the woman with him was a red head, and he used to teach her."

Annette continued to chatter. But the spell was broken. All of Alice's senses were alert. A former student of Sam's? There had been some rumors years ago. Annette had stopped, dried Alice's hair, and began to untangle it. She sprayed some conditioner on and cocked her head.

"Do you want it shorter in the back?"

"No. I like to put it up for the season," Alice managed to mumble.

Had Alice heard it right? Was Sam seen with some young red head– and when had this become just another story about him?

Fully engaged now, Alice found herself forcing her breath to slow down. The effects of her moments under Annette's magical hands had evaporated. What was left was that old sense of the ongoing saga of Sam and Meghan. Her imagination was fully engaged.

"So, Sam. He still has some listings here on the Lake?" Alice asked.

"Some. He is still asked to show properties. He must be avoiding Suzy, I would imagine. But he lives up north, now. Lizzy, my sister figures that he has someone else already. Poor Suzy," Annette added, "she is still hurt."

Time had passed. Meghan too had been away. Summer seemed ages ago now . Was Meghan aware of Sam's doings, if any? Or was this just Sam with a potential buyer? Innocent enough. It was the reference to a student that irritated Alice. Why bring up something from so long ago?

Alice didn't pursue the topic further. Annette blow dried her hair and moved onto topics like favorite holiday recipes. Alice focused on the smiling Santa just over the mirror before her. But her face showed a reddish tinge. Annette sprayed her hair.

"I love Party Mix. I add additional pretzels, cheerios, and nuts to mine," Annette offered.

"Yes. I add cranberry juice to the kid's ginger ale. For color," Alice responded mechanically.

Would the holidays change everything for Meghan, Ed, and Sam.? Did the time away bring in new interests? Cold snow was on the ground. The lake remained empty of kayak rides and outdoor walks.

Alice paid Annette and added a generous tip. As she left the warm, moist air of the shop, bitter cold air hit her face. Her eyes teared. Someone's heart could be broken this year. And someone else's must decide.

On her drive back to the lake, the colors of Christmas seemed somewhat muted by the icy coat of winter snow. She drove quickly down the plowed roads, around the corners, and down past the camps along the lake shore, hardly glancing at the tiny tree perched merrily on her neighbor's porch.

CHAPTER 15

"December 6, 1917"

Alice felt dreamlike. How had she driven herself back to the lake in such a state? Christmas cast a spell on her, and this year seemed to be an especially intense one. Was it just her sense of protectiveness towards Jack MacNamara's daughter? Had Alice let herself become too invested in Meghan's personal affairs? Annette's customers reminded Alice of her own Canadian past; the familiar sound of French had her mind returning to family members, especially her own grandmother. She would always love the smooth sound of French rolling off someone's lips.

Noticing that the red flag was up on their mailbox, Alice pulled over and got out to collect her mail. Their metal box barely peeked over the banks. So many boxes would not survive this winter, being toppled by the plows.

She pulled out a collection of flyers, cards, and bills. Red, green, and golden envelopes fell from the open box. She seemed to send and receive fewer cards every year, but old friends and relatives faithfully dispatched their holiday wishes, and Alice loved to read them.

She sat back inside her car and perused the stash. Post marks were from Arizona, California, Connecticut, and Colorado. Then there were a mix of postcards and oversized cards stamped England, Canada, and Ireland. Bob remained in contact with people she barely knew. He would want to open some of these himself.

Holding up one envelope, Alice scowled. She had to get in touch with her siblings soon. After the first of the year was soon enough. She was aware that she had been avoiding them for months. It was easier to immerse herself in Lake affairs than to get involved with all that it would entail. She tapped the corner of one card and put in on the bottom of the pile. Why ruin her enjoyment of the holidays now?

She paused to examine the various organizations that sought her donations. This time of the year there seemed to be so many good causes. The children's funds and cancer usually won her heart. But December held a special charity for her.

Closing her eyes, Alice leaned back against the seat of the car holding one large folder tightly to her chest. Tears welled up. Again, she could hear the clicking sound of Grandma LaFrance in her ears, and then the soft roll of her tongue as she pronounced her r's. Alice pictured the family kitchen smelling of the crust of pork pies in the oven. Tourtiere they were called. These meat pies were a part of every *Le Reveillon de Noel* that Alice could remember. How did the children keep their eyes open so late? Was there nothing like the taste of her aunt's caramel candy?

But it was during Alice's time spent in cooking French sweets that she would learn what the real family stories were about. The elders would speak of December 6th among themselves, certain not to spoil the celebration for the young. But Alice heard their muted words spoken in the kitchen. She would carry their stories long after her bedtime and sometimes have nightmares as well. They did not know just how curious Alice was– or how much she could understand from their quiet French whispers.

There had been a horrible accident in Halifax on the morning of December 6th, 1917. In the Narrows, two ships collided. One held explosive materials headed for the war effort in Europe. One ship was going too fast. They had passed on the wrong side. Residents saw smoke and heard explosions, and instinctively rushed to the harbor to see what was happening. Only the crew knew what was really at stake but were unable to be understood in the confusion. Children stood in front of glass windows to look. That was what remained for Alice.

In one moment, two thousand would die. Nine thousand would be severely injured. Glass would lacerate and blind. Two hundred would lose their sight. Bridget LaFrance's uncle was one of them.

While most Americans remember December 7th for Pearl Harbor, Canadian hearts recall the day horror struck their quiet community. It was the worst man-made disaster before the atomic bomb. The LaFrance women wore something black throughout Christmas in memory of the day, recalling horror and heroism. But Halifax was not forgotten.

Alice wiped her eyes. How was it always so much worse when children were involved? And so close to such a holy time for French Catholics. Throughout Alice's life, whenever she would encounter anyone with a visible scar or blindness, Bridget La France's words would softly say- 'Don't stare. It's the explosion.'

Bob was approaching the car and waving at Alice. She waved back.

"Hey, thought you were volunteering at the library, today," he hollered.

Alice smiled back. She really was in a fog that morning. She realized that she had driven right by the library and come directly home. Quickly, she sent the ladies at the library a message on her phone, and then started her car. Bob waved and headed into the camp, his arms full of groceries.

Her eyes returned to the tree sparkling on Meghan's porch. Again, she could picture another tree, much larger. For almost a century, the people of Halifax remembered that day with a similar gesture.

Upon receiving a telegram that Halifax needed medical assistance, Boston had sent a relief train full of hundreds of nurses and doctors. There were as many as twenty-five thousand who had lost homes. But the injuries would fill medical journals for years after. Eye injuries were among the worst.

Every year since, Halifax had sent a huge fir tree to the people of Boston. It is lit at the opening of the Christmas season. The bond between the two countries was forged. Neither would ever forget the tragedy or the goodwill.

Alice placed the envelope that would hold her seasonal gift; her eyes fixed on the tree again. Such a small gesture between two countries so long ago. Someone had thought it an appropriate gift here.

Whoever it was who had left the evergreen, Alice liked them even more.

CHAPTER 16

"The Start of a Season"

With the day to herself, Meghan decided to add to her 'to-do' list. Max was in good hands with Bob Finch. She needed to make several stops. Simplify. She kept telling herself. But when was Christmas ever simple?

The service at Ben Franklin Ace Hardware was great. The clerk wrapped up a perfectly shaped tree for her and loaded in into the bed of the truck. She would use the metal stand she had dug out of the shed. Dad's glass ornaments would work as well. Tiny white lights intertwined everywhere would add a certain charm to the mantel piece, and to the indoor tree. She was able to locate colored lights to replace those burnt out on the old string. The short limbs that the clerk trimmed off the lower part of the tree would make the perfect garland. Luckily, it all fit in the truck. The red truck itself created quite a picture with the tree sticking out almost a foot beyond the tailgate. She hung a red ribbon on it for safety.

Her next stop was in Manchester. The mall had been busy since Black Tuesday. She never did get into shopping that day despite all the inviting sales. *Let Thanksgiving be Thanksgiving*, Jack MacNamara used to say. And so, she knew that as a result she had to squeeze a lot of shopping into fewer days. The parking lot looked full.

The last time she had spent time at the mall was when she purchased her summer clothes. This was not the season to try on bathing suits. Where had the summer gone? She felt this more and more often. December was no exception. Mentally, she thought of who she wanted to give gifts to.

Sears remained the perfect place to pick up some baby items for the Campbell twins. She knew to buy things a size bigger than marked. And of course, doubles of everything. She added two blankets and Christmas bibs. For how many generations had Sears dressed America's families? Meghan remembered when her aunt used to pour over the old Sears Roebuck catalogs. There was always one lying around among the magazines. Times were changing. She herself had even begun to order things through Amazon. Still, it was nice to roam and collect cute baby clothes. She spotted a pair of miniature denim overalls and red sweaters she just had to buy for the infants.

She promised herself not to get distracted. Arms full, Meghan glanced at the holiday outfits displayed on the mannequins. That would have to wait. The list of events taking place in Hampton Hills looked inviting and she would need to find appropriate clothes. Just not today.

Drinks were her next item. Champagne and wine were on her menu. Kevin would bring more wine. They weren't much for mixed drinks in the MacNamara household. But a bottle of Bailey's Irish Cream was traditional. There was a New Hampshire Liquor Outlet near the hardware store. Once inside, Meghan had found what she wanted to have on hand; she laid the bottles on the floor of the passenger side. She'd added a bottle of rum in case they made punch.

The Dollar Store proved to be the most successful stop. Full of ribbons, candles, assorted ornaments, and candy, Meghan filled her basket. She could use some items for stocking stuffers. She grabbed some stockings for the kids just in case. Wouldn't they expect that Santa would need some place to leave the small items?

By mixing the old decorations with the new, she would create a camp with a Christmas feel. They might make some too, so she decided to add two pairs of small scissors, a bottle of white glue, sparkles, and a package of colorful paper to her growing collection. Already, she could picture her kitchen the center of a holiday workshop. She knew handmade decorations did what old and new ornaments could never do. And her small guests would be kept amused.

Her cart was brimming with Christmas as she rolled it toward the cashier. It was already getting dark in the lot. Her red truck did resemble Santa's sleigh, she mused. So many memories yet to be made and what better place to make them than on the Lake this year?

As she drove east on Route 101, the Uncanoonuc Mountains lay grey against the dimming light. A deep orange belt crossed above black clouds, a sign of good weather. There was little to remind Meghan of the recent autumn with white covering trees still heavy with leaves. To her right, a breeze lifted one loose leaf, it danced as if on a white stage. Winter had its grip and would not let go for many months. She tuned into an FM station and listened to holiday music. The heater hummed away warming her feet and face. She found herself smiling.

Mountain Road appeared on her left. A thin line of white outlined the sign for Pawtuckaway State Park. She turned her car between snowbanks, the road much narrowed. Tips of limbs overlapped above her. Lights twinkled from dark homes that lined the road. Summer felt far away.

"Christmas is here." She said aloud.

The tree in the trunk bed rolled to one side as Meghan drove down onto Clayton Shores Road. With her load, the camp would forget all about sunscreen, wet towels, and boat cushions.

She lowered the window to get a better view of the spot where her mother's birdhouse had hung. The void was evident. And Ed Shea's face passed before her. She needed to call him for, among other things, the tree sitting on her porch. The lake came into view, matte gray and frozen. But the tiny tree winked and invited her to come inside. A sudden warm rush of summer passed over her. Ed was such a part of her time here. Despite the clinging leaves, the setting sun, and the snowy blanket, Meghan was doing her part to fully engage with winter, but summer and fall thoughts lingered everywhere around her.

And the tree remained silent with its secret on her porch.

CHAPTER 17

---◦━❖◦❖━◦---

"Faces from the Past"

Alice Finch glanced at her face in the rear-view mirror. Annette delivered a good haircut. In her state of mind, she hadn't really taken a good look at herself. It would do (for an old girl, she liked to say). Apparently, this old girl's mind needed something to focus on. She had turned her car around and headed back into town, the librarians expected her, even if she was a little late. It was a good thing that Meghan was not at home and so she wouldn't be tempted to say anything about Sam Norton. Staying detached for now remained her promise to herself, even if it was killing her.

Flicking her bangs back, she counted the cairns along the road. There seemed to be more of them as some of the snow melted during the mid-day sun. The radio blasted carols as some stations were playing twenty-four hour Christmas tunes from now until December twenty-sixth.

"I saw mommy kissing Santa Claus," was playing as Alice hummed along.

So, Sam Norton's life on Winnipesaukee Lake was already reaching here and coming under scrutiny in their town. Alice's curiosity about the red head wasn't the only thing on her mind. He was free after all. But what did Meghan know about him since their time spent teaching together so many years ago?

"Silly tune," she said. " Who had Sam been kissing lately?"

Soon, the bulky outline of the Hampton Hills Public library came into view. Alice glanced at the dashboard clock; she was an hour late. The clock in the town office confirmed it. White lights shone in office windows and along the first floor of the library. They kept them on all day for the children. She was heading there.

Oversized wreaths also hung from each window. A giant red ribbon hung along the sides of the large oak front door. She drove behind and headed in the back entrance, a short cut to the Children's room. She hoped that they were not waiting for her. It was her usual day to read.

"Hey, Alice. So glad you made it in. We were worried with so many of our regulars canceling. Two of the ladies fell. One broke her wrist. This ice!" The tiny brown-haired woman they referred to as Birdie, called out from behind the check-out desk.

Alice smiled and headed toward the back corner where her preschoolers would have congregated. Alice had a dozen holiday-themed story books ready to go. She had set aside others on the effects of winter on hibernating animals, and some on the Festival of Lights.

"Alice, may I ask you for a favor?" Olive Smith called out.

The sprightly librarian seemed to have appeared out of nowhere. She stood in the middle of the Children's room, a look of concern on her face.

"Sure," Alice replied.

From the look of the room, few toddlers had come for the reading hour that day. One girl sat waiting, her mother nearby. It was not unusual for one of the parents to take over. The mother of a small boy volunteered to read to them both. Alice and Olive thanked her.

"I need you upstairs," Olive began.

Olive led Alice up the marble stairway that led to the balcony. Alice liked the view from here. She could see the alcove below where she had done her Halloween fortune telling only weeks before. But today, she would be helping organize, always an ongoing job in small libraries.

"We have some classes coming in to work on a history project. We are trying to pull out topics of interest for them to look over. The teachers want them to utilize primary sources and so put their hands on actual documents and evidence."

Alice nodded.

"What we are trying to do is to make it interesting even though it involves some research. It is so hard to compete with computer files, but these are not available any place but in our archives. At least not yet."

As Olive explained she held her arms wide over piles of folders, boxes, and books spread on a long oak tabletop.

"The students will be working in groups for a few days. They are to create a fictional story out of facts. They will invent the characters, but the stories must be based on actual places, people, or events that occurred here in our community. They can draw, make up songs, as well as dances. The story could have happened. These short plays will be presented after the first of the year. These sources include all kinds of local history," Olive explained.

Alice was impressed.

"So, I am cleaning up the resources for them and making it a little easier to find this information. Right?" Alice inquired.

"Generally, they can be as creative as they want. The goal of this is to make history more alive. And in the past, the kids seemed to have had some fun with it," Olive explained further.

Olive left Alice with a chair and extra folders. She also pulled out some empty boxes. They were already labeled- 'People, Places, Events, Weather, Occupations, Other.' Alice rolled over a chair and a filing cabinet on wheels. She grabbed a file and began to sort it out.

For the next two hours, Alice found herself immersed in images of Hampton Hills. Before her were pictures and accounts of dirt roads, horse drawn carriages, dairy farms, grocery prices, ice harvests, Model T cars, and period fashions. She carefully placed each article, note, photo, or account in the corresponding folder. Soon, the piles in her movable cabinet filled. Names of generations of familiar families passed her hands; Gove, Sachs, White, Mooers, Brustle, Meindl. She found an article describing the arrival of a local circus in town. Hours passed as Alice lost herself in the local life. She was reminded how much of this information might be helpful to Meghan as she completed her own family story. Alice would direct her here.

Alice had sorted almost seven boxes and decided to do one more. She was hungry and usually only stayed until noon. This box was on a trolley, so she rolled it over to her workplace. The box held mostly official records. There were dates of deaths, marriages, births, town anniversaries, and graduation lists. It must have come over from the town offices. One folder contained the pictures of soldiers from town who had died. Many faces were of the early founders of the area. She placed each in the proper pile.

The students certainly had a wealth of content to work with among all of this, she thought. They would basically be writing their own 'Our Town.' Such a clever way to encourage interest in the past. The many names and faces felt alive to her as she filed them under their contributions or their life stories. The dates were gradually coming closer and closer to modern times. She was now entering people who were born in the 1950s and 60s into her collections.

Opening the last folder in this batch, Alice realized that it focused on graduates from Alan Shepard High School. More names sounded familiar to her. One pretty girl had left town and become a successful actress. Another young graduate joined the air force but lost his life flying planes in Vietnam. The faces looked back and out at the world; like all youth they, looked stared forward hopeful, innocent, and fearless.

As she filed and sorted, she moved into her own times. And the face of one graduate looked very familiar. She double checked the date and figured that the person must be related to people she had met here in town. The file was not as faded as the others, appearing to have been added more recently. Then it struck her. The young man depicted in this file looked just like Sam Norton. But it wasn't him.

She stared hard. This person could not be this young on this date. It was too young to be Sam, but it sure looked like him. She placed the photo on the table and did the math again in her head.

"You must be exhausted. I forgot you were still here. Thanks, so much for all your work," Olive's voice broke her trance.

Alice looked up and smiled blankly at the librarian. Picking up her hat and coat, and slipping the photo inside the outside pocket of her oversized bag, Alice placed the last folder into its appropriate file. Slowly, she stood and headed toward the door. Olive closed the door behind them and shut off the lights.

As the two women descended the long stairs, Olive went on to express her appreciation for Alice's continued help.

"Oh, no problem. So interesting," Alice managed to say.

Minutes later, heading toward her vehicle she patted the outside of her bag. Alice was not a thief. What had possessed her to take the picture?

There was something very odd about this discovery. Rumors were one thing. This was something else entirely. She intended to find out the truth once and for all.

Pictures did not lie.

CHAPTER 18

"Local Facts"

Olive Smith headed back upstairs and sat down where Alice Finch had just vacated. Alice had made a lot of progress. An enormous pile of local history had now been digested. The history of Hampton Hills was impressive; it celebrated its three hundredth anniversary soon. With the town turning to its past, many residence had donated to the collection in the library. Olive wanted to revisit more of this and continue filing it into better order. She planned to have it become computer accessible next. This school project was another reminder of that, and any steps in that direction helped.

Local interest in a town's past ran in trends. The entire country seemed intent on tracing their roots lately, and Hampton Hills was no exception. This teacher picked up on the trend and by adding an element of creativity, had stumbled a unique way to not only teach history, but allow teamwork and a drama piece to the assignment. Olive liked teachers and had once considered becoming one. But she did not enjoy speaking in front of large groups. Although working in a library was allowing her to get better at it. Picking up one of the last folder in Alice's rolling files, she ran her fingers over the contents. Her favorite person, Ed

Shea, still had the folders he had picked up at the end of October. She'd sent him reminders, but he may have not received them. Many people remained without internet service on Pawtuckaway Lake since the snowstorm. She would snail mail him another one. Hadn't Meghan O'Reilly also requested similar information? She had seen Meghan in town recently. Olive wanted to let Meghan know that the information was due back soon.

Olive lifted the top from another box. She had overheard a police officer once admit that until he worked on the force, he had no idea what went on in his hometown. He didn't elaborate, but these records clearly told many tales about their small community. Towns had their secrets. The last box held news clippings of unsolved mysteries that had occurred locally.

The church bell had been stolen in 1912. No one ever found it. Someone put a cat in Santa's sleigh one Christmas parade. There had been several unexplained fires, toppled statues, tipped cows, papered town offices, and reworded business signs. On one Fourth of July, fireworks were let off inside the courthouse. On a more serious note, Hampton Hills had six murders. The articles assumed that the guilty parties must have been outsiders. And then there were the missing persons.

Ed Shea's file had pertained to one such case. He seemed interested in a man who left town around the early 1930s and never returned. Olive Smith wondered if her old principal was becoming a sleuth in his retirement; he'd been very secretive about his research. Had the man in question been a relative of his? Olive liked the folders on marriages and births. People picked such funny names in the past, she thought. And the photos of seated women in tight-necked dresses with severe, mustached husbands standing behind them, always made her laugh. It was sad to see the number of infants who died at birth, or the number of women who died alongside them. The old cemetery behind the library reflected these fatalities.

People interested Olive. She looked forward to what stories the students would invent and which facts they would choose to include. An old iron served as a paperweight on one unfinished pile. She wrote 'miscellaneous' on it and added a small milk bottle to keep the thick file closed. She felt that there was plenty here for the kids to dig through. Olive closed the door to the archives room and shut off the hall light. She headed toward her office to fill out a mail reminder for Ed Shea, and a note for Meghan O'Reilly informing her that the materials she wanted would be available soon. It occurred to her that both were essentially looking into one family– the MacNamaras. Many families discovered that they shared similar ancestry back in the old country. Genetics remained a popular hobby. There were just a lot of people, of many ages, digging through the same information that Alice had kindly arranged for them. Olive felt proud at how the community made use of her library. She would do her best to provide them any help she could.

CHAPTER 19

—◆•◆—

"A Boyish Fish Tale"

"Dad, he isn't sick. He's faking it," Kate stated as a matter of fact.

Ed held the phone away from his ear. Could his daughter hear him snicker? What boy wanted to be in school just days before Christmas? And with all this snow awaiting him outside?

"He doesn't have a cold, sniffles, snuffles, sore throat, or a tummy ache. Hot chocolate is his solution," Kate added.

Ed listened to his daughter's efforts to convince him to support her.

"Look, Dad. Danny has a writing assignment to do. It's due on Monday, December 15th. There are only ten days left before Christmas. If he comes up to visit you at the lake, he'll *never* get it written."

Silence fell. Ed's heart was with the boy. Kate would be up in a few days, but his grandson really wanted to stay with Ed when Kate went up North to sell his finished birdhouses. Danny usually remained with a neighbor. Holiday craft fairs scattered all over Winnipesaukee Lake this time of year and Kate needed to deliver her items.

"Look, Kate," her father began, "We'll get his paper done. I promise."

Ed winked at himself in the mirror above the fireplace. He really hated this skipping school as a principal, but this was his grandson. Thank goodness Kate couldn't see his face. He wasn't being much help to her.

"Okay. You promise, Dad. He has other projects to do too, but this one has to be done for *this* Monday," she emphasized the day.

Four hours later, Dan stood outside Ed's door with a duffle bag and backpack. Kate loaded up the dozen colorful, almost Norwegian looking birdhouses stacked in cardboard boxes, into her trunk.

"You men have one assignment- write that composition!" Kate ordered as she kissed them both. "It must be five hundred words."

"Sell, sell, sell," Ed ordered back with a broad smile.

"These are so festive," Kate commented, "All these houses need are some goldfinch, sparrows, or red cardinals."

Kate headed for her car and turned to wave. As she sped up the hill, her car disappeared in the snowy branches. Ed and his grandson hauled the bags inside.

"Let's have cookie and milk," Ed began, "We need to talk about this assignment."

"Grandpa, what can I write about? Everybody else writes about dragons and vampires. I don't have a dog to tell a story about. How do you just *make up* a story?"

The boy moaned as he nibbled his still-warm oatmeal raisin cookie and sipped his milk.

Ed poured more milk into his glass and sat back wondering the same thing himself. Creative writing had never been his thing either. He liked facts.

"Danny, we'll figure this out," Ed sounded much more confident than he felt.

An hour later, as Ed and Danny crawled into Ed's jeep, Dan had an idea.

"Grandpa, remember your friend at the library?"

"Yes. Olive."

"Can't we go see her? It's right near the market. I could look at some books and maybe get ideas."

Danny remembered their research back at Halloween. Ed had his doubts, but it was worth a shot.

Both warmly bundled up in a scarf and woolen hat, Ed drove them into town. The spirit of the holiday permeated the heated interior of the jeep. Danny commented on the lights dangling across the streets. He hummed merrily to the holiday tunes playing on Ed's car radio. Ed wasn't sure that he could bear to hear 'Jingle Bells' sung one more time, but Danny seemed delighted.

"First, the market," Ed decided.

He parked the green jeep close against the snowbank.

"Can you get out?" He asked Dan.

"I think so."

He squeezed his small frame between the door and the frozen wall of snow. Once out, Ed produced his list.

"Mom makes lists like that too," Dan commented. "I think it keeps her from buying too much chocolate."

Ed thought of Joanne. His wife found any excuse to buy Hershey's kisses. The two men quickly noticed that the aisles were full of holiday treats. It was difficult to stick to the list with so many temptations. Danny watched, as many customers greeted his grandfather, stopping them to comment on the weather, school events, and upcoming town festivities. His mother often remarked that having Ed for a father was like being related to the mayor. Danny enjoyed it and listened to all the conversations.

"This is my grandson, Dan. He is up for a visit," Ed introduce him.

Back at home, nobody knew them. He liked feeling a part of Hampton Hills. He felt like a special guest too. He was very helpful as Ed selected food for dinner and added extra items for Dan's visit. Danny knew that Ed didn't eat all this food when it was just himself.

Ed checked off his list- hamburger, beans, apples, oranges, bananas, and grapes. He tossed in Jiffy Pop, some Hershey's bars, a pint of vanilla ice cream, and a package of special edition cranberry English muffins. Additional packs of spaghetti and sauce were soon added. Some green beans would add vitamins. The rest he felt he had enough already at camp. Somehow, the list always grew with Danny along. And this shopping was part of the experience.

The two pushed their full carriage up to the cashier. The clerk, of course, knew Mr. Shea and wished him seasonal greetings, nodding at Dan as he loaded the bags. Danny helped load it all into the back of the jeep.

"To the library," Dan announced.

"Okay. Let's give it a go."

Once inside, Ed and Danny headed upstairs. Ed stopped to respond personally to Olive's emails, and to let her know that he had received them and would drop off the files that week. He needed to make more copies. Danny paid little attention as grandpa stalled on his overdue materials; he was distracted by a group of noisy teens arguing over some article they had found among the mound of folders strewn across the long oak table. The Archive room was buzzing that day. Ed nodded for Dan to go ahead in.

Dan sat at a small table with a book he had found and started to look through the table of contents. The book was about New Hampshire oddities. Surely, he would find something to write about here. But the commotion among the students continued to make it hard to concentrate. He began to listen to what it was they were so worked up about.

"It's not true. Someone made it all up. No one can prove it. I don't believe it," said one loud boy.

"It is too. My uncle saw it himself. He said it was like a pet," another replied.

"There are no pictures," one girl pointed out

"They saw it with their own eyes."

"The teacher won't allow it."

"I won't do it."

"I vote no."

The book in Danny's hands included a chapter on Mystery Hill. It was in Salem, New Hampshire, a real place. He couldn't use it. His paper had to be imaginary. But he liked the idea and tried to read about it. The noise continued as the group of teens tried another option. The folders were scattered everywhere. A librarian nearby looked up from her desk but said nothing.

Ed had wandered up and was approaching Dan. He saw his grandson who appeared to be buried in a book. Dan got up and returned the book, continuing to watch the group. Suddenly, the group dropped their files and headed out the door. He headed over to see what they had been so intent on.

"Can I look here?" Dan asked Ed.

"I think so."

Picking up the folder in question, Danny carried it back to his spot. He opened it and began to read a story about a tame bass fish that lived on Pawtuckaway Lake. The writer claimed that this fish lived under his floating raft and ate shiners from out of his hands. This fish lived there for years.

Was this fiction? Truth? Fantasy?

Danny loved the story. He wanted to believe it. He could add to it, couldn't he? In his story, he would swim with it. He would call it by name. He would feed it cheese. He would save it from being caught. He would call it to the surface.

When Ed came over to sit with Dan, he found his grandson smiling broadly.

"Find something?" Ed inquired.

"Sort of," Danny hesitated, "do you believe in tame fish? Like a pet who lived on Pawtuckaway Lake?"

He waited, expecting Ed to mock his story.

A twinkle grew in Ed's eyes. He didn't argue. He couldn't lie. He did not deny the story.

"I'll give the fish a name. I'll write a whole story about it," Danny said with excitement.

"Okay, son." Ed nodded, "Just don't mention the man in the article by name."

"Why not?" Danny wondered

"Because in these parts, his name is Herb Borer. And for many of us, his story is real."

CHAPTER 20

"Many Hands"

Olive Smith was a native of Hampton Hills. She observed and absorbed people and surroundings well. And of course, Ed Shea held a special place in her heart, and not just during Christmas. He had, after all, helped her get this job. And more than that, she admired and trusted him. Quiet, but astute, Olive had been very aware of the chemistry she had seen between Mr. Shea and Ms. O'Reilly. She wasn't in the classes they taught but had both of them for study period when she attended Alan Shepard High. And Sam Norton made Olive uncomfortable. All the other female students adored him. But she felt that he had flirted a little too much with the pretty females.

Rumors surrounding attractive teachers was common. Didn't every high school have it? Some rumors reflected the natural sexuality of teens who saw romance everywhere. There were faculty members who dated one another, and the teens gossiped about it. Sam Norton was young, fun, and energetic. He was bound to raise suspicion. But Olive remembered one rumor concerning a student named Janine. Janine was not shy like Olive had been as a young girl. Janine wore stylish clothes, heels, and makeup to school. Most of the girls did not. Janine had contact lenses when only Hollywood actresses had them. And Janine seemed to require a lot of extra help from Mr. Norton. But that didn't make a high school crush a crime

The folders that Mr. Shea had asked Olive for contained a lot of old records that included births, deaths, and marriage dates. They were for this family heritage project he was working on. He claimed that he was tracing his roots to Ireland. He had kept them past their due date, but much library material was forgotten during the snowstorm. He had promised to return it all so Olive wasn't concerned. The only part of his request that puzzled Olive was the folder about the MacNamara family. That would be Meghan's line of history, not his. True, many Irish traced their roots to the same town or county. Galway seemed to be of common interest to local historians. But Mr. Shea also dug into some student files, ones he might have had access to when he was the principal. He wanted more yearbooks, especially those from 1975 through 1990. He seemed interested in personal stories, like the files that she had set out for the upcoming students to peruse. What would such information have to do with tracing family roots? Olive had made a mental note and wondered at the odd direction Ed Shea's interest had taken. The school would have more than she had, but he had come to her to find it.

As she refiled and sorted documents, she kept out what she thought Meghan O' Reilly would find useful . Olive had sent Meghan an email that some of the requested information was back. Some local news was among the mishmash of files that her volunteer, Alice Finch, had helped organize. She had no way of tracing DNA, and some locals went online in the library to contact companies that did this. There was clearly a lot of overlap in such a small town, and Olive knew all those doing the research.

Olive pushed the last file inside the oaken file cabinet that Alice Finch had been working on. Soon, she hoped that much of this data would be recorded and be computer accessible. She needed some financial assistance for such an undertaking. The library remained underfunded. Olive really appreciated her volunteers. It just seemed odd that her archives room was unusually busy lately. Was there a pattern here? Was is just her imagination? The same thoughts seemed determined to fill her mind. When she could, she might double check the contents herself, she decided. It wasn't her nature to question why people researched things. But this time it did seem rather coincidental to her

CHAPTER 21

"A Familiar Face"

"Oh, my God," Alice shrieked.

The tall snowbanks and Christmas lights were distracting and making driving in downtown Hampton Hills hazardous for her. Or maybe it was the photo burning a hole in the side pocket of her bag that kept diverting her attention from the road.

That young man in the photo sure looked a lot like Sam Norton. Only Sam was too old to be getting some athletics award for a high school sport in the 1990s. Mr. Norton taught at the high school with Meghan in 1974. The boy in the picture was no more than eighteen. Alice could not reconcile the two. It made no sense. Minutes later, Bob heard the car bumper hit the edge of the curb. Snowbanks made it difficult to find landmarks. Their mailbox leaned at an odd angle. The plow driver could not have seen it under the snow and pushed it too. Only recently could any driver determine where roads ended, and sidewalks began. Bob glanced up while dragging a carrier full of firewood, headed for the living room. It was difficult to use one hand with his fingers still wrapped. He wasn't one to baby what he considered a minor injury.

Alice literally hopped from her car. He could see the pompom on her hat above the banks. She was moving fast. From her speed he knew she had something to tell him. A trip to Annette's usually involved some bit of news. Gossip. But no one called it that. He wondered what she had heard.

"Nice haircut," Bob called out.

In fact, he could seldom tell the difference. Alice was not one to alter either the cut or color radically. Alice said nothing, nodded, and headed straight inside for the kitchen counter. She carefully placed her big purse down, staring at it for a split second before tossing her keys inside.

"Hungry?" Alice asked.

"Yeah, I was just thinking I would like to eat something," he replied.

He left the small logs inside the door of the living room and headed for the counter. He pulled down a loaf of whole wheat bread from the cabinet and placed two slices on two Christmas themed paper plates. Automatically, he filled the kettle with water and turned on the burner. Alice had said nothing, so he waited. She laid a wax paper package full of turkey out, placing a jar of mayonnaise beside it, and ripped off a pair of lettuce leaves. A small pitcher of milk emerged from the refrigerator. Like synchronized swimmers, the couple prepared their lunches.

"So, how is Annette?" Bob finally asked.

"Good. Her place is just overflowing with holiday cheer. She had on those goofy antlers with bells."

Alice found a sharp knife and cut the sandwiches into halves.

"Bob, do you remember those rumors about Mr. Norton? You know, when he was a science teacher over at the high school," Alice began.

"Vaguely. The usual stuff of teenage girls. Why do you ask?"

"Want cukes, pickles, or chips?"

Alice's focus remained on lunch.

"Pickles."

Alice was stalling. She clearly had some piece of news that she was processing. He knew this from years of observation. He also knew not to rush her.

They made their way to the table, sandwich plates in hand. The water boiled and the pot whistled. Bob poured hot water over the teabags inside two pottery mugs; they tipped in some milk. Alice glanced at the counter, her eyes penetrating the side of her purse. Bob took a bite of his bread.

Suddenly, Alice reached over and pulled her bag toward her. She slid something out and placed it face up in front of Bob. He glanced sideways at a photo of a young man in a basketball uniform. The number sixteen was embroidered on the front. Above the number were the lettering for Alan Shepard High. The face looked familiar.

Bob paused and reached for his glasses. He looked more closely at the image.

"Hmm," he commented.

Alice choked as she gulped down too much tea.

"Who is it?" She asked.

Bob stared hard. He picked it up and then placed it back on the kitchen table.

"Looks like a picture of Sam Norton. Why?"

"Look at the date."

Alice pointed to the writing on the edge of the photo. It read 1990.

"It can't be Sam. But doesn't it look just like him?" Alice asked.

"It does. Where did you get this?"

"A pile of stuff at the library."

Alice looked away.

"You stole it from the library?" Bob smirked

"Borrowed. I borrowed it."

Alice bit off a large chunk of turkey and wiped off an invisible crumb from her lips with her red paper napkin.

She stared at the picture before them without further comment.

CHAPTER 22

***

"Time Flies"

"Dad, how did you and Danny come up with that whole fish story? Danny got an A!" Kate's voice was rich with pride. She chuckled at the feat. It had been a week since she and her son had been up to see Ed.

"It's a true story," Ed replied softly.

"Sure, it is. A pet fish? Come on," Kate shot back.

"Hey, I heard that story all my life. They fed it. It swam around their dock and raft. It lived there for years!" Ed sounded hurt.

"But it didn't come when they clapped their hands. It didn't jump over buoys. They didn't actually swim with it like tame dolphins."

"Well, no. It was after all, a creative writing assignment. Danny took some poetic license with it. But, Kate, it is a part of lake lore," Ed added with a snort.

"You and Dan are a pair."

It was all Kate could think of to say.

"Thanks. He is really thrilled with his grade. No one else wrote about a fish."

Ed was looking forward to the upcoming visit with his daughter and grandson. They would spend the week of school vacation with him. He had been busy digging out long-forgotten decorations, tree ornaments, and linens. He'd moved a chair to make room for the tree.

"I'm putting lights in the windows facing the lake," Ed added.

"We are looking forward to coming," Kate admitted.

"Do you remember the white porcelain reindeer Mom had?"

And for the next few minutes, Ed and Kate recalled past Christmases-onion dip, Chex mix, cranberry relish, Hershey's chocolate kisses in shiny red and green wrappers, and all the effort Joanne had put into decorating the house. Kate could picture hanging up her stockings and leaving out cookies for Santa. She remembered photos of her taken for Christmas cards. Some included their dogs. They had had beagles and poodles over her lifetime.

"Of, course, Dan isn't going to admit his disbelief in Santa. He likes it all the way it is. He wouldn't want to spoil it, or hurt your feelings," she added.

Ed could be heard to take a breath. Since when was his small friend worried about ruining it all for his grandfather. Didn't time fly?

Then Kate remembered something she'd wanted to ask her father.

"Dad, you know when I worked part-time in the town market last summer?"

"Yes."

"I met most of the town there. Everyone came in for something because we were so much closer than the supermarkets."

"I know."

"Well, there was this guy, older, but nice looking. Sam, I think everyone called him. He was at the Pawtuckaway Family Day. Remember? He arrived in a boat and gave out balloons?" Kate explained.

"Yeah."

"Well, I swear I saw him up in Wolfeboro when I was delivering bird-houses. He walked by the store and I got a quick look at him from inside the gift shop window. He seemed quite distracted by this attractive red head he was with. But, I swear, he's the same one from Hampton Hills," Kate said with conviction.

Ed thought for a minute. How much should he admit to knowing?

"He lives up there now. He is a real estate agent on the big lake," Ed tried to sound non-committal, "At least that's what I've heard."

"Wasn't he engaged to the lady all dressed in white, the one distributing the balloons?"

"Yes, he was. They broke up."

"Well, I don't know anyone in New Hampshire, so it just struck me that I would recognize someone up in north country," she added.

Ed made no reply.

Kate dropped the subject, satisfied with the response, and went on to comment on just how picturesque the drive up Route 93 was. It was like a post card, just spectacular with trees still burdened with snow. Wolfeboro could be called Santa's village she observed.

"We have one of those. Remember when Mom and I took you there?"

Ed tried to follow Kate's conversation after that, but his mind had drifted elsewhere. Copies of the papers contained in the library folders lay on his desk. He had finally returned the originals. Olive had kindly allowed him to keep them days after their due date. They contained scattered information that tied into the minor scandal related to Sam Norton. Most of that information was locked in the old files in the basement of Alan Shepard High School. But there were birth records. They were public. And the odd newspaper article or photo. There was a paper trail that someone could follow. He had. And there it all sat with him still wondering what to do with it.

Principal Ed Shea refocused on the chat at hand and asked Kate what Dan might like added to his wish list for Christmas. When he hung up a few minutes later, he could not recall anything she had just said. His role as protector of local families remained even after retirement. Every town had its stories. But in this case, so much of this one pertained to Meghan MacNamara O'Reilly.

CHAPTER 23

"If Walls Could Speak"

Emails came and went on the Finch's computer. Meghan had yet to get computer service and had to visit next door to send and receive her messages. Alice didn't object. It was a good excuse to visit with Meghan. But the days were busy ones. Meghan was engrossed in her plans for the upcoming visits and spent her time making the camp reflect the season. Sam appeared busy with another listing that involved staging an enormous old estate that sat on waterfront property on Lake Winnipesaukee. Their exchanges remained casual and mostly chatty. Alice saw no reason to be concerned about the romance since she saw no sign of Sam's car in the driveway. And she had a good view of it from her bedroom window.

Standing in the doorway of the camp, Meghan admired the decorating job she'd done so far. She had utilized the red plaid pillows from the upstairs room and relocated them to the couch. They complimented her red buffalo checkered napkins and tablecloth. White candles placed in brass candlestick looked alter-like on the mantelpiece. Meghan scattered old tree ornaments into the string of garland beneath them, hiding the wooden shelf above the hearth in rich greenery. From the top shelf of the kitchen, Meghan retrieved four holiday mugs, adorned with reindeer and snowmen. She would use the white pitcher and red bowls for dinner ware. The linen closet proved to be where her mother had stored a large glass punch bowl. After a good cleaning, it sparkled. For now, it served as the container of red apples, seedless grapes, and navel oranges. It sat as the centerpiece on the plaid-covered table. In a brandy snifter, she placed a white votive on a bed of cranberries. The rest of her decorating utilized items she'd bought from the local dollar store.

Using her bag of silver snowflakes, Meghan created a chandelier, and hung it from the frame of the ceiling ladder. With the lights off, it almost looked as if it were snowing. Tommy and Beth would love it. From the same store, she purchased two stockings which already hung ready on the damper handle of the chimney. All in all, the camp had been transformed to her satisfaction. The brown cardboard box retrieved from the shed allowed her to add some small signs of Christmas to the bedrooms and bathroom. Still, it seemed that the MacNamaras had more. This was only a fraction of what she remembered. Had Jack finally cleaned out much of it? When Sally died, he would not have wanted it all. Much of the old decorations must have ended up at a rummage sale, she decided. Why else was she unable to find any more? Her final touch would be setting up the tree. That could wait until her family arrived.

Meghan headed down the hall toward her bedroom. She flopped on the bed and faced the ceiling. She could not think of anything either red, green, or sparkly that she could put out as a useful sign of festivities. Simplicity was not a bad theme. Closing her eyes, she could conjure up some of her own decorations, sitting in her attic in Arizona unused. This place didn't feel quite done yet. Sitting up, Meghan positioned herself in front of the mirror on the bureau. She intentionally lined up the photos of her parents that were stuck inside the frame of the glass. Last June when she had first arrived, she discovered that she could see herself and them together if she sat just so. She smiled at them in the mirror

"I want you all here," she whispered. "I want it to feel that all the MacNamaras have returned to the lake this year," she said to their images. The room behind her looked different reflected in the mirror. She noticed how crooked the curtain rod looked above the bedroom window. The image of the room was all backward and the pattern in the knotty pine walls seemed off. The largest knots on the wall resembled a face with two knots as eyes and one as a lopsided nose. It didn't appear so face-like when viewed head on.

That was when she noticed something. Jack had rearranged the furniture in the room to make himself a reading corner. He had shoved one bookcase off in a corner and pushed another at a right angle. In doing so, he had blocked much of the wall near to the window to utilize daylight when his floor lamp wasn't necessary. Meghan could almost picture him there with his reading glasses on, and the face of the wall looking down at him. She got up and looked directly at the same place. Nothing unusual, and yet...

As she looked more closely, she noticed that one of the knots in the wall was not a knot at all. It was a small black handle that blended into the background of the woodwork. Walking toward her father's little book niche, she could also make out black hinges near the handle. Finally, she could see upon closer scrutiny, that there was indeed a small built-in cabinet half hidden behind the corner bookshelf. She gently removed as many books as she needed to lighten the heavy oak shelf and pushed it away from the wall. She took the small handle in her hand, pushed down on the lever, and the door opened. Sure enough, a narrow series of shelves had been built inside. She started to cry. Lined up carefully on the shelves were the tiny porcelain statues of their old creche. On the top shelf was the wooden manger and beneath were Mary, Joseph, the infant, donkeys, camels, the shepherds, and wise men. One by one she carried them over and placed them on the bed.

On the remaining shelves, wrapped in linen tea towels, Meghan discovered glass snowmen, a set of *NOEL* lettering, hand blown tree ornaments, Celtic crosses, a crystal angel, and brass window candles. The last shelf contained four time-worn stockings with the names- 'Dad , Mom, Meghan and Kevin' embroidered on their faded fronts.

Everything had been there all the time. Someone had stashed them in there; who would have remembered? Was it Sally? Or had Jack himself decided to store them there? All her life, Meghan had never found out where her parents hid gifts. Sitting back on the bed to position herself with them, she laughed. The

Lake continued to tell her much about herself and her loved ones. The spirit of Christmas continued to haunt these walls. She scooped up her treasures and began spreading them all over the rest of the camp, feeling that the walls had spoken.

CHAPTER 24

"Stories from the Past"

Alice could be heard. Doors opened and closed loudly. Things were dropped and retrieved with deep sighs. Scratching sounds of paper came from the attic. Shivers ran up Bob's spine. He compared the annoying noise to fingernails on a chalkboard. He and Alice needed to disclose what they had learned. He had already left Ed Shea three voice mail messages with invitations over for supper. So far, no reply. It was driving Bob and Alice crazy. On the south end of Pawtuckaway Lake, Ed could make out the bare boards of Dolloff Dam. He had spent time that morning perusing the website of the 'Pawtuckaway Lake Improvement Association' and all the oral histories recorded there by Jeff Gurrier. Hadn't Ed's own father known many of those interviewed by Jeff? The lake had its own history made from so many who had discovered it deep in the woods of New Hampshire. But tonight, it was the other stories that troubled him. And some stories were best left in the past.

Ed Shea was the steward of many personal mistakes. So many of his former students had left Alan Shepard behind and entered fields like law, medicine, technology, and the military. What happened in their teens was not necessarily a bell weather of future accomplishments. Some had also endured many hardships and left town to begin anew elsewhere. He had heard from many, over the years, after they graduated. He knew intimately about their plights and victories. The lake protected many stories indeed. Danny had loved the tale of Herb Borer's tamed bass. He wanted to know more. Had there really been rabbits on Rabbit Island? Did a mini-tornado hit the lake in the 1960s? Who was buried where the cross sat at the intersection of Meindl and Brustle road? Ed had become caught up in his grandson's curiosity. Telling the lake's tales brought up Ed's dilemma concerning what to tell and what to withhold from public scrutiny. Ed's concern was laser focused on two men: Wil MacNamara and Sam Norton. His own family research had resurfaced buried evidence on both men. Who was *he* to expose them now?

Each time Ed replayed the multiple voice messages from the Finch's, he felt more strongly about confiding in them. Alice really did have a sixth sense about such things. And Bob had a heart of gold. Ed's Irish ancestry was full of luck charms and Celtic signs. And his soft spot for Meghan made it all the more important to assist her as she crossed the threshold into family secrets. From Ed's perspective, Meghan's happiness was tied in with both men. And this made it even more difficult for Ed to be objective. He had to put personal feeling aside. Ed sat down at his computer. He checked the weather. His own internet service had only recently been reconnected. Christmas was just days away. There would be many holiday events, including the craft fair, snowball dance, community chest of giving to the Salvation Army toys for tots, and the traditional visit from Santa. Holidays historically held conflicts with excitement and anticipation on one hand, and demons and sadness on the other. The key was to be busy with it all . Enjoy the best and leave the rest. Everyone deserved to absorb the spirit of the season.

He reached for the phone. He needed to talk to his friends. A dinner at their home would be the perfect setting to open discussion about everything on his mind. All this information had come to him, after all. He needed some feedback. What should he do with it? And when? They would know what he should do.

CHAPTER 25

"A Reckoning"

Alice added a red velvet ribbon to the evergreen wreath she'd hung on the front door of the camp, quickly closing the door behind to keep out the winter cold. Bob had finally been able to clear the porch, allowing her to hang a matching wreath on the nail above the porch window. Inside, a white candle burned brightly in a red lantern. She smiled at the effect of her artistry; decorating was an intricate element to her seasonal enjoyment. The place looked welcoming.

The smell of baking ham filled her nostrils, with an added aroma of pineapple and cinnamon. She referred to this dish as Hawaiian Pig. It was a favorite of Bobs. There would be leftovers for sandwiches. Bob stood beside the sink mashing onions into his Yukon potatoes. Cabbage steamed on the inside burner of the stove. Dinner rolls awaited their turn in the oven. Ed Shea was due any minute. They were ready they thought. Absently, Alice opened the drawer next to the flat, silver refrigerator. She closed it quickly. The photo of Sam Norton's look alike stared out from the dark interior as if from a coffin. She shivered. What an image. But she *was* bringing back something from the dead. Should this long buried rumor be left where it was? She remained disturbed by it all.

"Grab me the milk?" Bob asked.

Alice quickly opened the refrigerator door and poured about a quarter of a cup over Bob's mixture. He quickly sprinkled pepper over it and a generous pat of butter. Alice saw him add a tablespoon of sour cream. He was going all out on his mashed potatoes that night.

Alice returned the milk to the shelf and lifted a jar of mint-apple jelly. Ed Shea was very fond of this with his ham. Alice's French Canadian father liked his ham this way too. It was hard to find it, but they looked for it this time of year. Along with another seasonal favorite, pepper jelly. They said little and moved together preparing the dinner. Each one lost in their own thoughts about how Ed would react when they brought up the topic of Sam Norton. And so, they were both startled to hear the loud pounding of feet in their front porch as Bob shook snow from his boots.

"Hello," Ed hollered.

Alice and Bob exchanged a quick look. Alice headed out to where she had just hung her wreath and to where Ed now stood, hanging his coat on the hooks behind the front door. He'd removed his boots and stood in gray rag wool socks. A loaf of bread nestled under one arm and under the other appeared to be a bottle of red wine.

"Well, hello, stranger. So good to see you," Alice said as she accepted his offer of the loaf.

He kissed her on the cheek. She hugged him warmly.

"Come in. We're almost ready."

As they passed through the living room, Ed paused to admire their tree.

"Nice tree. Good shape."

"Thanks. A bit shorter than usual. I could reach the star," Alice replied with a grin.

They stood for a minute. It was a blue balsam. A white star sat sparkling on the top. Strings of popped corn and cranberries wrapped the tree's branches. Assorted decorations hung in between tiny white lights. At the base, a deep red and forest green quilt skirted the trunk. Alice liked the look. Some of her decorations were decades old.

"Did you make this bread. It feels warm."

"Yes. It's pumpkin with walnuts."

Ed headed for the drawer to retrieve a knife for his bread and a corkscrew for the wine. He knew this kitchen well and was familiar with where most things were. He had had dinner here many times. It felt like home to him in many ways. The three of them worked together easily.

He pulled out the draw where the corkscrew was usually stored. Looking inside, he stopped short. Sitting on top of a set of nutcrackers and just to the right of the corkscrew was a photo. His hand pulled back. He pushed the draw back. Alice and Bob said nothing. Ed re-opened the drawer and picked the photo up with one hand. With the other, he retrieved the bottle opener.

Alice stopped and watched Ed. Bob turned from the sink and waited. Ed placed the photo down and began to open the bottle. For a minute no one spoke.

"Where did that come from?" Ed finally managed to say.

"The library," Alice replied softly.

Again, a long pause.

Alice took three wine glasses out of the cabinet and handed one to each of them.

"Shall I pour?" Ed asked.

"Let's retire to the living room?" Bob said in a formal tone.

Without a word, the three left the kitchen, glasses in hand and gathered in front of the burning fire. A large plate of assorted crackers and cheese sat invitingly on the coffee table. Just as they approached the couch and chairs, a loud bark sounded from the porch.

"Max," Bob stated and quickly left the room.

Ed and Alice faced one another. Ed held the photo and carefully placed it on the edge of the table. Neither spoke.

"Max, no," Alice said firmly.

The dog headed immediately for the appetizer plate which was just at his eye level. Alice quickly removed it and put it on the sideboard adjacent to the television.

They gathered near it and stood nibbled on the cheese.

"So, this photo you have. It was in the library," Ed began.

Bob nudged Alice on her left arm, nearly spilling her wine. She stepped away and lifted the glass to her lips.

"Yes. It was in the archives. I was organizing files for Olive when I found it. We have been arranging folders for some students who are working on a school project. There is a lot of stuff that needs to be sorted and she asked if I would help."

They all stared at the photo. It sat alone on the empty table, a distance away. No one bothered to bring it to where they stood.

"Who is it?" Alice finally burst out.

Ed looked toward Bob for assistance. Bob averted his eyes and watched Max find a spot to lie down in front of the fireplace.

"Who do you think it might be?" Ed answered in a low tone.

"Looks just like Sam Norton- a really young Sam Norton," Alice volunteered.

They waited.

Bob sat down and picked up the picture.

"It is and it isn't," Ed replied.

"But the dates. They don't gel. Sam was a teacher by then. Maybe, he had already finished teaching. This is a replica of him, isn't it?" Alice went on.

"Again, you are half right. "

Ed sat down next to Bob on the couch. Alice sat on the tweed chair to their right. Each took a long sip of wine. Max gave out a long moan. A log crackled in the fireplace. Ed gazed down on the photo and back at the faces before him.

With great solemnity, Ed began.

"I am surprised that there is a picture. The boy was not with us for long. His mother moved back with her mother briefly, and the boy attended Alan Shepard during her stay. He didn't come to the graduation but did receive his last credits from here."

Ed related the rumors surrounding Sam Norton and the former student, named Janine. According to Ed, she was out of school by the time they got together.

"She was an adult. Whatever flirtation happened while Sam was her teacher must have picked up later. We think she had this boy. The dates coincide," Ed went on.

"So, this is probably a picture of Sam's son," Bob stated.

"Most likely."

Ed looked out over the lake water. "As long as Sam taught for me, only the usual schoolgirl crushes seemed evident. I had no reason to assume anything more. Mr. Norton was a good teacher. He and Meghan both had Janine in their classes. But Janine was more mature than teens her age. She was attractive. There was no father and her mother worked full-time out of town."

Alice and Bob listened without interruption.

"What most likely happened, occurred after Janine graduated. The records seem to indicate about six years later. I have the proof. Sam may have married her for a brief time, to give the boy a last name. The marriage didn't last. The boy would be in his thirties by now."

Ed got up and moved toward the sideboard to select another piece of cheese and cracker. He broke the cracker in half and headed back to the couple who had not left their chairs. Max followed and stared at them. He gave up and returned to his spot before the fire.

Bob looked over at Alice.

"How long have you known?" Bob finally asked.

"I suspected for years. The boy's attendance left little in doubt. He was not in the yearbook. But this athletic photo would have been taken by the newspaper. He was a good ballplayer. Only delving into my family records, did I get sidetracked and find the birth and marriage records. Frankly, I don't know what to do with it all," his voice drifted off.

He sat down and finished off his glass of wine. Alice got up and refilled it.

"Who else do you think knows this?" Alice inquired.

"Very few. It wasn't important. And it really isn't now either."

The smell of something burning reached their nostrils. Alice quickly left the room. Max followed her to the kitchen. Bob stood and the men faced one another.

"But it is important. Isn't it?" Bob offered.

"Only if it impacts Meghan," Ed replied.

"Yes, I agree. My feelings exactly," Bob nodded gravely.

CHAPTER 26

"Hallmark Moments"

Carefully, Meghan continued to unwrap the items found in the narrow cabinet. Each one receiving the appropriate pause. The creche looked right on the table in the front window; she was surprised that the entire assembly was still intact. She located an angel and three sheep tucked inside the wooden structure. Her hands trembled as she set them in the order that she had seen Sally do- camels on the right with the wise men, shepherds on the left with the sheep behind them. How was it that she remembered such a thing? Other hands had placed them here. As an afterthought, she strung tiny lights around the window frame and stepped back to admire. The family creche had survived with only a few chips in the paint. The walls had kept them safe.

For over an hour, Meghan unwrapped other decorations someone had so wisely stored behind the wall. Had they been there before Sally died? Or did Jack refuse to touch them once she was gone? The shelves held years of memories for Meghan. Along with the tiny red tea towels with green wreaths and set of *Noel* wooden letters, were a quilted angel, a Santa with a small opening for a light bulb, a porcelain Spode cup glazed with a tree, and matching porcelain candlesticks. She had carried them into every room and left one there. Every guest would enjoy her findings. The last item to bring back to life this Christmas would be locked inside Jack's green tackle box. They were tree ornaments. Meghan could barely see it in the back of the top shelf. Dragging over the ottoman from Jack's reading corner, she stood on tiptoe and maneuvered it to the front of the shelf where she could use both hands. It was where Sally and Jack had always kept their most fragile items. Without opening the lid, she carried it over to the bed and laid it on the quilt. With great ceremony, she pulled out the tab on the front and lifted the rusty top. It was all there. The tissue paper felt crunchy beneath her touch. Green, red, and yellowed white paper was peeled off to reveal slightly faded and often dented ornaments from her childhood. If Hallmark needed a spokesman, today it was Meghan. But what made the MacNamara collection unique was the use of bent fishhooks as fasteners. Most of the item retained their original hooks, just as Jack had attached them. There were over a dozen assorted ornaments, some badly soiled from moisture. But for this family, each was a reminder of a Christmas past and held special meaning. They reflected travels, hobbies, accomplishments, and benchmarks. One was from Kevin's first Christmas. One was to commemorate a trip to Ireland. Again, memories flooded her as she spread them on the bed. She planned to tell their story as the family put up their tree together on Christmas eve.

The tiny closet was empty. Meghan closed the door and the wall once again embraced it into itself. Stepping back and pushing the chair and shelves in place, Meghan stared at the photo next to the mirror.

"This was what I was missing," she told the images of Jack and Sally.

Suddenly, she realized that Max was not sitting at the bedroom door. When she had first discovered the cache, he had been sniffing the discarded tissue paper with interest.

" Max," she called out, "Hey, Max."

She had opened the camp door to use the electric outlet for her window decorating. He must have slipped out to do his business. But that was over an hour ago. She headed back to the front of the camp and saw that the front door was still slightly ajar. And there was no sign of him. She looked out in the yard in the direction of the Finch's, but the white landscape was empty. It was then that she noticed Ed Shea's winter jeep parked in the Finch's driveway. It was almost dark, but she could make out the outline. It struck her that she was usually invited as well when Ed was over. She felt a tinge of disappointment at the omission. Surely, she was a part of their gathering. Had she been intentionally left out?

She hollered in the direction of the Finch's.

"Max, come!"

Winter changed life on the lake when windows and doors were shut tight against the cold. If he was over at the Finch's, he could not hear her. She felt sure that her canine must have gone visiting. There was only one way to find out if he was there. She would have to call. With an attitude of slight indignation, Meghan picked up her phone and tapped in their number. It took only two rings when someone answered.

"Hi. It's Meghan," she said with authority.

"Hi, It's Ed," Ed responded. "Bob is pouring pineapple over steaming ham, so I picked up."

Meghan didn't feel quite as confident suddenly. The line was silent.

"Sorry to disturb you, but is Max over there?"

"Yes, He's right here. Want me to send him home?"

"Would you? I got lost in decorations and didn't realize that he was still out. Thanks."

Ed waited. Meghan waited. Bob glared at Ed. Ed shrugged his shoulders.

"I've been meaning to call you," Ed began.

"Me too," Meghan's voice came out in almost a whisper. "Since I got back, I've just been so busy with Christmas and all…." Her voice trailed off.

"Danny will be up with Kate," Ed managed to say.

"Kevin and Julie and the kids will be too."

"Then we'll be seeing you all in town."

"Sounds great."

Another pause.

"I'll send Max your way."

And with that, Ed hung up, leaving Meghan hanging on the other end of the line.

Alice returned from down the hall carrying napkins and an empty gravy dish. She found Ed standing with his back to her just staring into the fire. He seemed to be confused. He looked over at Max and walked toward the door.

"Max, go home," Alice shouted.

Ed opened the door to let him out, stepping out onto the porch.

Obediently, Max headed out the door and over the snowy yard toward the MacNamara's porch where Meghan stood with the door open to receive him. She waved at Ed and he waved back.

Bob and Alice exchanged glances. They headed for the table and began to pass the serving plates to one another. Alice headed toward the kitchen to fill her gravy boat. A large log fell in the hearth creating a loud thump. They all jumped. But no one brought up the name Sam Norton for the duration of the dinner. And the name Meghan too seemed off the table for now.

CHAPTER 27

"An Eyewitness Account"

The branches of a substantial Fraser fir scraped against the back window of Meghan's red truck. With the window cracked, she could smell the fragrance. The attendant was a wealth of information and had told her that this tree had sturdy branches, a strong scent, and shed minimally. It made her even more curious about the kind of tree she had sitting on her deck. It looked somewhat different to her, but she was no expert on evergreens and didn't know the difference between a fir and a pine. All she knew was that she liked the shape and the height.

It was the perfect size, she thought after examining rows of them. Between the found ornaments and the extras she'd purchased at Mr. G's discount store nearby; her tree was shaping up fine. She had a white star for the top and thought her son might be able to reach it without a ladder.

Why hadn't she had the sense to ask Ed about the tree on her deck while she had him on the phone? She was too focused on being left out of dinner and the awkwardness of the call. The mystery tree remained just that– a mystery still.

Piles of wrapping paper leaned against the passenger seat, along with ribbon, tapes, and tags. She had bought two bags of cranberries to string with popped corn. Her tree would be old fashioned.

She had been back on the lake almost a week and had only had email conversations with Sam. They hadn't yet had a live exchange. Hearing Ed's voice was a welcome sign that they were still connected at some level. But the feeling of disconnect remained long after she and Ed waved from separate porches at one another.

She could blame her erratic email. The electric company continued to work with local utilities to return electricity to homes. Many cell towers were damaged in the snowstorm. Olive's efforts to contact her were heroic. The librarian had left her a voice mail message, and sent her a post card, telling her that her requested information was in and that she could come by to look at it. Meghan wanted to have all the information at hand and remained determined to complete her family album by Christmas. Her next stop was the library.

An entire season seemed to have slipped by between Thanksgiving and Christmas. Her time in Arizona cut the season in half. All the autumn signs of fall leaves and pumpkins had been replaced by snow and greenery. White lights winked from every window in the Hampton Hills library. Meghan admired the effects of the spotlight that shone on the face of the stone structure, illuminating a gigantic evergreen wreath hung on the front of the building. She parked on a side street then headed up toward the front doors.

So much sand had been spread on the granite steps, it resembled a beach. Meghan's boots dug into it as she climbed them. As she opened the oversized wooden door, heat hit her face. It felt warm and inviting as she stepped inside. And almost immediately, the smiling face of Olive welcomed her.

"Hello, Mrs. O'Reilly. Follow me," she said quickly.

Meghan followed her up the marble stairway to the balcony above. Olive chatted as they ascended.

"There has been so much interest in family history lately. It is a national trend. Do you know that I receive requests for former residents all the way from

Europe? I am so confident that the town will soon approve my request for a stipend to digitize all these folders into a convenient computer system. This is such an archaic method we have. Thank goodness for all of our volunteers who come in and organize materials to make it easier to find topics," she went on excitedly.

Meghan thought that Olive was a bit more talkative than usual. It was probably just the season. Didn't the entire town seem excited about Christmas? The holidays seemed to bring out the best in them. The season was evident everywhere. Even the railing going upstairs had been wrapped in yards of garland. Looking down Meghan admired a tall green tree that sat in the center of the lobby. As she ascended, she admired the dozens of ornaments on each branch .

The women approached a glass cabinet, set into an upstairs cabinet, from which Olive removed some folders. She directed Meghan to sit at a nearby oak table. At the other end of the table sat a silver-haired woman who looked up and nodded at them. The woman looked familiar to Meghan and as had become her habit, Meghan smiled back. So many residents were former acquaintances of her father. Meghan sat before the pile of folders and awaited Olive's direction. These were archives and were to be handled with care. Then, Olive directed the other woman to join them.

"This folder is primarily concerned with the years 1890s to about 1920s," Olive began. "Your family, the MacNamaras, seem to have been in America since the turn of the century. There are some records that date back to Ireland, like birth records and citizenship documents."

At first ,Olive said nothing to the silver-haired woman sitting with them. Then she began an introduction.

"This is Violet. She is one of our best historians here in the library."

Meghan nodded and shook the woman's hand. Olive continued to move folders nervously around on the table.

"This folder is more recent. It contains reports about the area from around 1890s until WWI. We have reports on the boys who left to go to war, families who lost sons. These carry us through the 1920s and the Great Depression. We have pictures of closed businesses here in Hampton Hills and Manchester, our largest neighboring city. This tells the story of the closing of the Amoskeag mills where many of our own people lost jobs. The last folder reveals the similar story of Lowell, Massachusetts, another big mill town. So, there is a lot of information stored here."

Olive seemed to be dawdling and rambling. What did all this have to do with her research into the MacNamaras? Meghan just sat and listened. At last Olive looked up at Violet and drew a brown folder from the pile. She nodded at her and glanced at Meghan. "Here is where Violet's knowledge comes in. She is the one to talk to about this," Olive stated flatly before rising and heading out the door, leaving Meghan facing a smiling Violet.

The woman got up and came around the table. She sat in the oak chair beside her and opened the file Olive had isolated.

"Did I meet you at scrap-booking?" Meghan asked suddenly recognizing her.

"Yes, you did. And the stories and pictures you presented got me thinking. Because, I have something to tell you that you will not find in your folders," she began slowly.

Meghan felt a slight chill. What could this woman possibly know about her family that Sally or Agnes had not? Did she have some story dating back to Ireland? Or was it a lake tale, one that an old fishing pal wanted her to know?

Violet touched Meghan on her arm and laid some newspaper clippings in order on the wooden surface.

"I had an uncle named Gerry," she began slowly as if not sure where to begin. Holding up an obituary, she noted the date.

"He died in 1980 after living a very interesting life. In fact, he would fill our heads with his adventures. His family worked in the cotton mills in Lowell, Massachusetts. When they closed, his family moved up to New Hampshire and lived in Manchester for a while. He was of Irish descent, and his address during those years was in what they called a "trinity" apartment on Bell street in the area known as the "fields." Gerry's father lost everything when his job dried up here as well. So, he, like so many, took to the road– or more accurately the rails. He was a hobo from roughly 1931 to 1933."

Meghan heard something familiar about this narrative.

"He met men from all over, unwilling to return home empty handed. Economics was the great equalizer. Uncle Gerry crossed paths with college educated men, foreman, tradesman, farmers and businessmen in his wanderings. They shared food, tales, and kept one another company out on the road."

Violet looked off into the distance before returning to her story.

"My Uncle Gerry knew a man named Wil MacNamara. They met on the railroad and got to know one another. Apparently, he and Wil picked up and traveled for a time together."

Meghan shifted in her chair. She stared at the women unable to believe that here might be the piece of the puzzle she had been trying to solve for months. She needed more information about Wil and his sudden disappearance. Was it possible that this was a lead?

"Uncle Gerry told us about an incident that took place in northern New Hampshire one night. He and his companion had hopped off a train, and were following the tracks. This was one way to stay traveling in one direction. Uncle Gerry called the man Willy, and as they talked, they both realized that they had left the same area in Manchester. They exchanged all the news they had, as did most of the men. Your grandfather revealed an old news clipping that he had been carrying, and of course they began to reminisce about their former lives here. At that moment, they decided that it was time to go home– with or without money. So that was their plan."

Violet stopped.

Meghan was riveted. This was not a tale she had ever come across anywhere in her research.

"Did your uncle come directly home? What year was this? Did Wil MacNamara change his mind and stay on the rails?" Meghan's voice was soft and weak.

Violet took a deep breath and looked over Meghan's shoulder as if seeing something. She fidgeted with one of the folders and then folded her hands on her lap.

"The local papers reported that Wil's body was found along the riverbanks of the Merrimack."

She placed the news clippings in front of Meghan and waited to continue. But Meghan just stared at the headlines and waited for Violet to go on.

"These are the articles that tell the story. One implies that it was an attempted suicide."

Meghan picked up the articles and scanned them again. Still, it didn't feel right. Why would this woman want to tell her all this? It all seemed surreal to her. Was this why Jack wouldn't talk about it? And why would it matter to know all this now? Violet touched Meghan on the shoulder.

"There is more," she said softly. "The papers just had evidence. They reported it was a head injury from falling. My uncle had his own version."

Meghan had hardly moved. She realized that she was squeezing her hands together so tightly, it hurt. Her eyes went from the headlines of the local papers, back to Violet.

"According to Uncle Gerry, one night a few of the hobos stopped on a trestle. One of them traveling that night was injured. They had stopped to lift him off and get him onto the road just on the other side of the river. You do not linger on a trestle. Well, they felt the vibrations that indicated that a train was coming their way. Willy picked up the man and tried to carry him off. Many of the other men ran, and some just jumped into the cold water knowing that they could not make it to the other side before the oncoming train. The train swept past as many watched from the shore or from the waters below. When they all met up on the opposite shore, Wil was missing. He had apparently thrown the injured man to safety but was forced to jump where there was no safe landing. He must have hit his head on the supports below, killing him instantly. But he saved that man's life."

Violet sat for a minute and waited for Meghan to process all this. She folded the articles inside the folder and patted the front cover. Meghan sat in silence.

"Your grandfather was on his way home. Uncle Gerry made it back. But he never forgot Will or his act of courage. The newspapers had not gotten the story right at all. But now you know," Violet said softly. Tears ran down both woman's faces. All the voids in Meghan's project made sense. Sally and Agnes's persistence had not been in vain. The mystery of Wil's disappearance was finally solved. An eyewitness was there. The post cards had stopped. Wil MacNamara had been heading home, just did not quite make it.

The women embraced each other just as Olive returned to lock up the room. Meghan hugged the folders to her chest as the three descended the staircase.

"Thank you," Meghan said to Violet and Olive.

"We just thought that you should know," Olive admitted. "This is the true story to complete your family tale."

Meghan drove back to the lake a bit shaken. She had a story to finish– and an ending she could never have imagined. She wanted to tell someone what she had just learned. She felt as if she might explode with such news.

But who?

CHAPTER 28

---•◦•═►◄═•◦•---

"Nocturnal Visits"

Meghan's tree bounced merrily in the back of the red truck. The folders carrying that news of Wil were tucked under her down coat. She had maneuvered the road leading toward Clayton Shores with little attention to the twists and turns, her mind still reviewing all that she had just learned. This new piece to the family story changed the narrative, both creating shocking news and rewriting the ending. Could she keep it all to herself until the unwrapping of the album? Her insides still burst with it all.

Through the bare trees, she could already make out the lights of the tiny tree perched on her deck, and the outline of the camp. Automatically, Meghan turned to face the tree where Sally's birdhouse used to hang. A pit formed in her stomach. Was she just hungry? She realized at that minute that she wanted to call Ed. He would know what to say. He always had.

She drove through a tunnel of snow covered branches as she turned down the last hill, and headed down toward the camp. Her eyes caught the blocked edge of the driveway. A familiar vehicle sat next to the porch. It was Sam Norton. She parked her truck beside him. He stepped from the vehicle and waved with both arms. A sense of shyness washed over her. Then she looked at this handsome man in his royal blue winter hat and another emotion surfaced. Before she could define anything she was feeling, he opened her door and wrapped her in his arms. Their lips met. She looked into his face and his eyes sparkled back.

"Nice tree. Let me give you a hand with it," he offered heading for the back of the truck.

The large brown frame of Max suddenly appeared from over the top of the snowbanks. He headed toward Meghan almost toppling Sam as he struggled to lift the tree from its bed.

The world felt right. It was like a scene was from a Christmas card. Wasn't this what she wanted?

While Max ran circles around Meghan and managed to jump up and place a wet kiss on her face, Meghan collected her packages from the truck.

"Didn't you get my messages?" Sam inquired. "I was in town. The roads are cleared and so I had snow tires put on. I could actually drive down your road!" He said teasingly.

He pulled the tree up the stairs and on to the deck.

"Cute tree," he commented absently nodding at the small evergreen.

Meghan waited for him to say more.

"Someone left it there," she hinted.

"Could you hold this door open for me?" Sam asked as he tried to balance the tree and the screen door. Max pushed by them, racing inside.

Meghan quickly presented the awaiting stand she had found in the shed to Sam and, together, they stood the tree into it, securing the metal screws into the trunk. As she filled a pitcher with water to fill the stand, she offered Sam a cup of hot chocolate. Max patrolled his bowl in anticipation of his dinner.

"The place looks quite festive. I like the buffalo print pillows," Sam observed. "Very LL Bean."

She smiled and pulled down a can of powdered chocolate and a small bag of marshmallows she had been saving for her grandchildren's visit.

"Let's get some lights on this tree," Sam offered enthusiastically.

And so, he began to unravel the strings of boxed lights Meghan had recently purchased. She opened the bags of cranberry and supplied them both with needles and string, and they sat together, two cups of hot chocolate steaming before them.

"The entire lake is ready for the season," Sam continued. "All the storefronts in Wolfeboro are chuck full of lights, ornaments, cards, music, and gift ideas. Downtown is impassable; it is so hard to see with the snowbanks piled up so high. And of course, ski season is in full swing," he added.

Meghan listened as he caught her up on his latest listings, the price of lakefront properties, and all the damage done in north country from the Thanksgiving storm. She felt herself calm down as she half listened. Her mind returned again and again to the demise of her father's father, Wil. It was a secret yet to be told. Why did she not seem to want to tell Sam?

He was obviously delighted to be here with her. He face was slightly tanned since he had already gone skiing this season. His voice had always soothed her, and his manner charmed. She was just not truly present.

"You're kind of quiet," Sam said, awaiting a response. "How was Arizona? Will you be selling it?" He inquired looking directly at her.

"I'm really not sure. I just had to return to assess the damages it had received from the storm that they had faced. My place was lucky. And when I returned, there were no frozen pipes or collapsing roofs here either," she responded in a kind of jumbled way.

Sam had sat. Now he got to his feet.

"I'll pop some corn. We can eat as we string," he offered with enthusiasm.

She helped him find the kernels, oil, and pot. As she waited for the oil to heat, he headed for the fireplace and crinkling up some newspapers from a nearby pile; he began to prepare a fire. He wandered out to the porch, to the stack of kindling he had noticed, carried some in and soon had a blazing fire going. Meghan pulled out some ham and cheese, pickles, and chips. Sam found mustard and a bag of cocktail carrots. The two stood at the sink and rinsed out wine glasses Sam had spotted in the kitchen cabinet. Meghan set out Christmas plates and matching napkins. She opened a bottle of chilled Merlot. Soon the three were settled on the couch in front of a warm fire; Max curled up as close as the grate would allow to warm his ample behind. Sam and Meghan nibbled on the buttered corn and sipped wine. She caught him up on her trip to Arizona and casually discussed the latest on her family.

A sense of calmness and peace swept over the scene. Sam's presence had that effect on her. Hadn't she planned to put up the tree when everyone was there? She would wait to string the rest of the popcorn though. It was easier to do when the kernels were stale. The two removed ornaments from the cardboard boxes, and Meghan reminisced about each one. Sam listened attentively when she told him the story of discovering a hidden closet in her parent's room. He chuckled when she said that it was another mystery from her childhood– where their gifts had been hidden for years. Darkness fell outside, but holiday spirit and congeniality brightened the world inside the MacNamara camp. Max snored softly. The effects of the wine and company set in. Sleepiness crept in too. The star on the top of the tree shown down on the scene. They all dozed off before the fire.

Bright lights glared in the window off the porch. Max jumped and barked incessantly at the sudden disturbance. He headed for the door, startled from a deep sleep. Meghan came to from some place back in time. Sam was sure he had heard a shot fired. Or was it the hammering sound coming from the outside door? Groggily, Meghan stumbled behind Max and peered out through the curtains. Three figures stood there holding flashlights. She opened the door slowly.

"Sorry, ma'am," a man in a uniform and hat immediately spoke. "We were just checking to see if you were alright."

"We received a call," the other official added.

"From the Fish and Game," the third man stated with authority.

"What is the matter?" Sam stood beside Meghan, the quilt from the back of the couch still draped over his shoulders.

"A bear was spotted in the area—with cubs," the tallest man explained tersely.

"Someone had been baiting. These bears are looking for food, been tipping trash cans. Yours is toppled."

The officer pointed in the direction of the road. Meghan could barely see beyond the tiny tree to make out torn black trash bags and food scattered over the surface of the white snow.

"We think they're gone, but you need to clean this up. They'll most likely be back," the second officer advised firmly.

"Yes. We will. Thank you." Meghan offered as she and Sam stepped back inside.

"Oh, watch your dog," one agent yelled as they left the porch and approached the cruiser parked behind Sam's white car. "He's a big boy, but mama bears are quite protective and unpredictable when they have cubs along."

"We will," Sam yelled back.

They pulled on their coats and gloves. Meghan put on her boots. Sam said little. For the next half hour, half eaten food, torn wrappers, and vegetable skins were collected and stored. They dragged the containers out to the shed, secured the tops and locked them inside. She would need to buy some tubs more suitable for winter or invest in some bungy cords to hold her trash lids.

Sam and she were wide awake now. Having focused on the emergency, the mood changed.

"Do your business," she ordered Max, "You're in for the night."

It was ten by the time everything had been done. They headed in. Max sat before the fading fire as if awaiting something. The air had somehow chilled inside. .

"Thanks, for driving down," Meghan found herself saying. She reached up and they kissed good night. She walked Sam out onto the deck.

🌲 🌲 🌲

Next door, a set of eyes watched a couple kiss beside a tiny sparkly tree. The white vehicle tooted its horn as it pulled out of the driveway and headed up the hill.

Bob washed his rubber gloves and set them carefully under the sink. They left their lights off.

"Max knows who the intruders were. He almost followed us back here!" Bob blurted out from restrained laughter.

Holding on to one another, the two fumbled their way off to bed, falling into each other's arms, giddy with their own charade.

"You're such a bear!" Alice chided.

And in moments they fell off to sleep, secure in the belief that an accident had been prevented. At least for now.

CHAPTER 29

"Falls in the River of Life"

Ed Shea watched clouds cross above the grayish-white surface of Pawtuckaway Lake. Those not familiar with the name found it comical, before wondering what it might mean. One translation of Algonquin was that it meant "place of the big buck." Others tried to say that it meant "land of sticks and stones." Ed had liked the second one because he believed the old adage that "sticks and stones can break my bones, but names can never hurt you." He had seen bullying where name calling, false claims, and rumors destroyed lives. His years as principal gave him ample opportunity to observe human behavior.

The first full fall of his retirement had offered him ample time to reflect and to choose what to hold on to. It wasn't just his years of collecting household items, birdhouse materials, and books that took up his attention. He had old files. Some were decades old. He felt that many families of children that attended his school were like relatives to him. These records held successes and tragedies, births and deaths, special events along with academic evaluations. Reviewing them told of awards, arrests, funerals, anniversaries, many of which he personally attended. They told of life in Hampton Hills with all its flaws.

Perhaps it was the size of his school that made his being principal so much more than just an administrative job. He'd served as priest, counselor, parole officer, and parent at times. Ed held these stories close to his heart. Files just held data. Behind them were real people.

Within a matter of days, Kate and his grandson would be coming to the shores of his lake home. Along with the season, many town family members came home as well. Former students, many parents themselves now, would stop him to wish him holiday greetings. Did they know or wonder what he remembered about each one of them? There was praiseworthiness and shamefulness there. All he had to do was turn the pages of the multiple year books stored in his home office or pull out a copy of a past Hills Report, the school newspaper, to remember the events through the years. What had become of their years after high school? Did it all add up to who they would become, or were there those whose lives took on odd twists and turns that no one could have predicted?

Ed was an old soul, his mother often told him. In her slight brogue, she would tell him that he was too serious, serious beyond his years.

"Don't carry the world on your small frame," she would say wisely.

He was born old. He never did anything without contemplating the outcome or consequences. He was responsible to his core. That sense of being the adult in the room did not vanish when he closed the door to the office of principal of Alan Shepard High. And so, all the evidence he had still needed to be handled respectfully.

The problem came when his intentions overlapped with his personal life. His research into his Irish roots had opened some information that paralleled with his work life. His family, the Sheas, had relatives who had worked in the Lowell cotton mills alongside the MacNamaras. Both families could trace their roots to County Cork and Galway Bay in Ireland. Story lines naturally fell in together. This was why he had wanted Ted to tell Meghan about the evidence he had on Wil MacNamara before she stumbled upon it unexpectedly.

Who could know what Jack MacNamara wanted his descendants to know? According to this account, Wil committed suicide. That was what the papers deducted. Sally had wanted records kept. Jack seemed to want to let it be. Who was right? What was the crime in leaving it all in the past, and to let Meghan tell her story without this black mark? When, if ever, did it need to be added to the family history?

For Ed, he was accustomed to being the safe port of records. He had a career of it as evidenced by the accumulated file cabinets he was sorting. His dilemma was if he was the right person to tell her. Ted had not said either way what they should do. But at least he knew about it. That, at least, was off Ed's shoulders now.

Ed had always loved Meghan MacNamara. His timing was off. He had so enjoyed their time over the past summer. Was it always difficult with those we love the most? Had he already missed his second chance with her? The facts surrounding Sam Norton were not for him to expose. Here he was crystal clear. He would not tell her what he knew about Janine.

Sam Norton was not good enough for Meghan. Even if Ed was far from being objective concerning this. If Sam didn't tell her about Janine, who would? But even in this case, the relationship occurred years after she had graduated. Sometimes, it was hard when you knew too much. Ed stared out at the frozen surface of Pawtuckaway for an answer.

The Sun broke overhead. Ed turned away from the window and pulled the curtain back in place. He knew teens who had lost their lives by drowning in those waters. But the lake did not ruin lives by reminding them all the dangers it held. Life went on.

Someone had once said that Pawtuckaway meant 'Falls in the river.' This one sounded right today. It reflected the way life often let people fall but survive. One bad fall didn't define a life.

Ed grabbed the file of copies he had on Sam Norton and his son. Looks were hard to deny. The photo Bob and Alice had, said it all. He gripped the folder tightly and, with undue force, threw it into the fire and watched it burn. Meghan must choose, not him. He would not influence her with this information.

He would see Ted soon. Perhaps, they would revisit the topic of Wil MacNamara. Meghan would find what she found. Until then, Ed would allow life to take its own course and he would remain the silent observer.

CHAPTER 30

"Openings"

(December 19, 2014)

Perhaps it was a result of Hampton Hill's sudden thrust into winter from Halloween that the feeling of Christmas was so intense this year. For many days slush, narrow sidewalks, and icy road had become the norm. There would be less gifts because no one had had much time to get all the shopping done. Many were grateful to have their electricity returned and warm houses to enjoy. As is the way of the New Englander, they would make-do.

Alice Finch had taken the liberty to update the seasonal schedule for the week before Christmas, crossing out old dates and inserting new ones. Hampton Hills' weekend of the 19-20th included the craft show, bake sale, Santa visit, snow-ball dance, and perhaps an abbreviated parade. She taped a copy of it on the inside door of the MacNamara camp. Max had arrived earlier, and the red truck was missing from the driveway. Alice surveyed the tiny tree on the deck and the remains of footprints around the trash cans from the night's adventure. She smirked.

"Max, would you like to be my spy?"

The image of Sam's son did not leave Alice's brain. Would he be back for the dance? They had only temporarily scared him off with their nocturnal caper. Bob knew the local police and of course the agent from 'Fish & Game.' They owed him a favor, he had claimed, and agreed to visit the house next door to warn of possible animal activity in the area. Alice felt it was the least they could do to stall the situation. But she also knew it had really been silly. She couldn't believe they had really fallen for a bear out of hibernation and hunting with cubs this time of year. The entire escapade caused her to chuckle again.

She crawled over the snowbank dividing the two properties, Max at her heels, stopping on the crest of the white peak to glance out on the cold lake surface. There was mixed icing along the edges, some residents had taken to de-icing around their docks, boathouses, and breakwaters. Bob and Ed had had long discussions concerning the real impact of the process and if it really protected structures from the damage of expanding and contracting ice. Men are good at talking about technical topics, she reflected; she wanted them to discuss Meghan and Ed's intentions.

"Men!" Alice blurted to no one.

Max paused and looked up at her with puzzlement.

Once back inside, the inviting aroma of warm chocolate filled her nostrils. She was making velvet brownies– hers with bits of cherries. She had made almost a dozen knitted scarves for the craft and bake table as well. Glancing over at her pile of colorful woven pieces, she remembered why she had managed to make so many more than her usual number. She kept her hands busy while Meghan was away in Arizona. To her they were "sanity scarves." She may have to make a few more even after the holiday season was over.

Carefully, she laid her tray of brownies on the counter. Max parked his wide behind on her right foot and looked up puppy-eyed. The smell must have been intoxicating to his canine nose.

"Sorry, Max. Chocolate is off limits for you. Did you know that it is poisonous for dogs?"

Max didn't seem interested in her reasoning.

119

"It should be defined that way for us humans too. Then maybe we wouldn't crave it so much."

He moved away and sat nearby watching.

"Come. Sit," Alice instructed as she offered him a dog biscuit from the jar next to the sink.

He sniffed it, paused, and accepted it, not one to refuse any form of food.

Alice headed down the hall toward her bedroom. She had the house to herself that day. Bob was joining so many of the other men doing their shopping. He'd left earlier heading for Manchester. It would have been more difficult to deny him a sample of her delicious pastry. She needed a dozen to look nice on her holiday tray. They would be covered and stored on top of the refrigerator, faraway from inviting noses and hungry hands.

Hung on the open door of her closet was her black velvet skirt. It was just long enough, with a slit up the side for easy dancing. 'Old reliable' she referred to it as, for it had seen many holidays. She'd found a new sparkly top and scarf to add to it this year. Slightly heeled shoes also in silver and gold would keep her feet from tiring too early. Add her diamond stud earrings and gold cuff bracelet, and she felt that she was dressed appropriately for the dance. She would have to carry her shoes and wear boots, and of course her long down coat and another woolen sweater would keep her warm while both going and coming back. Winter was still winter no matter how one dressed underneath.

It was always such a rushed season, she thought. Why not do Thanksgiving in November and then have Christmas in say, February. Now that was one dreary month. In the next few days everyone would hustle and bustle and end up with a cold. She had been so busy with the demands of the season that she had neglected even her own regiment of soup, tea, and some herbal supplements. After this month, she would get back to it.

Already, she knew that the Alan Shepard cheerleaders were planning to decorate the church hall as if for a prom. The hall would go from bake and craft sales, to visits from Saint Nick, to becoming the setting for an all-white room. She wondered if they would suspend snowflakes from the ceiling like they had done the previous year. Almost like a wedding, teens and dates danced alongside their parents that night. The little ones stayed in the church nursery, also cared for and entertained by local teens. Ed had had an important part in beginning this school involvement, and the high school encouraged the student body to volunteer.

"Max. What is that?"

The Golden must have been napping under her tree and picked up some tinsel. He dragged it into the room on his back foot. Alice reached down and pulled it off. She used very little of it anymore, but sometimes it slipped off from the top branches. It was on old tradition in her family.

"We need a ribbon on you," she offered again thinking about how the dog would be a great spy.

"So, what happened over there with that man?" She asked.

A frown came over her face. She wondered if both Ed and Sam would dance with Meghan at the upcoming event. Would Ed defer? Would Sam come with Meghan? The only way she knew that Ed was attending was because she heard him and Bob talking on the phone about it.

Ed wanted to know if Bob was wearing a jacket and tie. They felt that all this fuss wasn't necessary.

"Retirement is rough on my mid-section," She heard Ed complain.

He had to go and buy some dress pants. Alice had had Bob try on some of his and had let out the tucks she had put in two years before. It was the same for them all. Her velvet skirt had a nice elastic waistband. Despite her care with nutrition, her waist too was expanding. Only Sam Norton seemed to be escaping the effects. He looked almost as good as his son, she had to admit.

She headed back toward the kitchen.

She tapped the side of the pan where her brownies were still cooling and stuck a toothpick into one end. It still felt too hot to remove them in one piece. They needed to be perfect for the table.

She sat at the table and looked out the front windows over the lake. All before her was gray, black, and white. The wreath she had hung on the window frame blocked some of her view, but she could clearly make out the outline of the trees that edged the opposite side.

"What does go on inside the walls of those homes?" She pondered. "If walls could talk."

Max sauntered in from the bedroom and flopped at her feet. Absently, she reached down and pet his back.

"I really have to," she said aloud as she rose and headed over to where she stored her

Rune cards in the back of the kitchen drawer.

She decided to do a one-card reading. That was all. Just one card.

Closing her eyes, she held the pack and shuffled them three times. She placed the deck on the kitchen table and using only her right hand, cut it. She reached for the small box of matches and lit one of the candles in front of her. Solemnly, she turned over the top card- 'Openings.'

Alice breathed in deeply and breathed out. This card referred to matters of the heart. There was an image of a fire burning there. If any situation was dark, it would be clearer soon. Something hidden was to be revealed. She placed the card back in the deck and put them inside her velvet pouch. She looked out on the cold outside.

Only Meghan could know. Such a fine bit of advice in the darkest of seasons. Surely, light was what many searched for during this time of year. There was always some source of light in every dark place. And the best source was the heart. The light of the heart burned brightest.

Alice felt content. Despite the revelation in the photo, she would not interfere. Life would run its course. She would not try to sway events. Even if things went off in another direction.

CHAPTER 31

———◆·◆———

"Christmas Plans"

"Dad, how is your cold?" Kate inquired.

"It's just a sniffle, Hon. I'm fine. Alice suggested chicken soup and dropped by her own special broth, and as usual, it works wonders," he assured her.

"Is she doing any of her gypsy business at the Christmas fair?" Kate said softly.

"Not as far as I know."

Ed's voice sounded suddenly subdued as if the mention of the Halloween event wasn't one, he wanted to elaborate on.

"The spirit of Christmas likes to work its own magic," Ed added. "Your mother used to say that."

There was a pause. Both remembering something. Kate liked her father's friends, the Finches. Bob was like a brother to Ed. Had been for years. Kate hardly remembered Bob's first wife. And Alice seemed to mother everyone.

"So, Danny isn't being kept out of school today, but I will be picking him up early. We will be driving up to Wolfeboro first to deliver your last ten birdhouses.

They are the holiday versions. I saved another six for tomorrow's town Christmas faire. We should be done after that. I'll call you. Does that sound like a plan?"

Kate nodded in the direction of Danny, who sat before her doing math homework.

"That sounds great. Too much squeezed into one weekend, though. No wonder some of us get runny noses or sore throats this time of year. But it should be a fun time," he added with an excitement he didn't feel.

"I need to remember to pack my sparkly top and some fancy earrings," she said out loud to herself. "Did you find a suit?"

"Yes. I bought some new pants and a jacket."

In Ed's mind this qualified as a suit.

They both made notes about the upcoming days. Kate was bringing her cranberry-orange relish, sourdough bread, and an apple pie. They would need some sour cream, but she had a box of Lipton onion soup to make their traditional dip. Ed had chips.

Ed jotted down a note to remember to pull out extra blankets and his down covers. He would buy ice cream for the pie, and some soda water and chocolate syrup to make ice cream floats, later. The rest could be bought when they were all together- deli meats, cheese, pickles, cereal, milk, bananas, and other assorted foods. Christmas wasn't for another six days. He still had some last minute gift wrapping to do.

His mind wandered as Kate idled for a few more minutes. She discussed the road conditions, Danny's school holiday play, and his new ice skates. But Ed had already begun to wonder what else might happen in the upcoming days ahead. He decided that whatever it was, the most important thing was that Danny and Kate were coming. Children made Christmas. It always had for him and Joanne and Kate. Surrounded by family and friends was enough. He hoped to have a dance with Meghan though.

Kate got off the phone with her father. Something was off with him. Was it just retirement? Danny still looked forward to spending most of his school vacations up on the lake. Hampton Hills was certainly one town that knew how to celebrate the season. But she had noticed that her father was just this year. Even this cold of his was unusual for him. He had gotten a flu shot even.

Was Ed lonely? Kate's thoughts drifted to the O'Reilly woman. She and her dad had had a great summer together. He hadn't mentioned her in a while. Or was this something more? Maybe, he was spending too much time dwelling on the past with all his cleaning and sorting. Christmas lent itself to bouts of nostalgia for most people. And it was his first holiday after fully retiring. These thoughts nagged at her as she made Dan a snack.

Well, she and Dan would do their best to keep Ed's mind on the holiday at hand. They would keep him busy. He wouldn't have time to brood. They would all be together on Pawtuckaway Lake soon, and Christmas itself often cast a spell of its own.

CHAPTER 32

"A Slippery Road South"

Wolfeboro's main street, clogged with holiday traffic and skiers bound north, remained a favorite sight of Kate's. The Brewster Academy grounds looked quieter than usual, no doubt most students went elsewhere for their winter break ; final exams were over.

Cars moved like molasses past brightly decorated front windows; shoppers filled the sidewalks, barely visible behind mountainous snowbanks. Their arms were full of purchases. Black's Paper Store and Gift Shop sat sparkling in icicles and white lights, a Wolfeboro landmark.

"You can see where the Mount Washington docks," Danny announced over the now twenty-four hour broadcast of Christmas music that blared from the car radio. The ship was a favorite destiny for most coming up to the lake. Winnipesaukee sat frozen just beyond the town. No boats on the lake today.

He loved this trip.

"Hope we sell all of grandpa's birdhouses," he said wistfully.

They drove through town and headed up a hill past oversized Victorian mansions. Kate would choose a side street to park. She and Danny could carry the trays over to 'Tiny Places gift shop.' Among assorted garden elves and fairy tale toad stools, Ed's creations had found their niche. Customers seemed to love them. A line of customers already formed outside the door. Ida, the owner, smiled as Kate and Danny arrived.

As the two of them stepped inside, a set of brass bells tinkled above their heads. Warm fragrant air met their faces and nostrils. Free hot cider and chocolate sat on a table just inside the door. Applesauce donuts invited visitors to stop and nibble. Danny was there in a second to sample the sweets, gulping down two bite sized morsels, and grabbing a cup of steaming cider. Kate rolled her eyes and gave him a disapproving glance. Christmas was one temptation after another. The slight smell of cinnamon reached her.

They quickly arranged the birdhouses in the empty spots reserved for them. The tiny garden elves could almost move into her Dad's houses, as could a wide variety of bird. Kate could see that already Ed's display was selling well. There was no reason to linger, Ida had her hands full of sales. They headed toward the door, nodding at her, and slipped outside.

Dan stopped suddenly and turned to his mother.

"Mom, I need some time to shop alone," he stated firmly.

He looked at Kate with a look of 'YOU KNOW WHY,' in his eyes.

She understood.

"Well. Okay. But only half an hour. We need to head South. It's nearly six and the traffic will be nuts. I don't *need* anything," she added.

"I know. But I know exactly what I want to buy you."

Kate yanked on the front of his cap. She wanted to kiss him on his red nose but resisted. *Not in public* he would say.

"One half hour. Synchronize our phones. Right here. Okay?" She insisted.

"Be back then," he said, and took off down the busy sidewalk.

Kate watched his blue hat bob among the mufflers and disappear into the crowd. And for one split second felt that ache of his absence.

Was that how Ed still felt about her divorce? She was alone, as was her Dad. Did this concern ever leave a parent? She turned away quickly and headed for a coffee shop nearby. She would sit, read the 'Union Leader' newspaper and sip her favorite hazelnut coffee. The thought of a warm cranberry nut muffin sounded perfect to her as well.

At exactly six-twenty-five, Kate stood at the entry of Tiny Places, still sipping her coffee. She focused on the direction that Dan had gone and stared like a dog expecting him to return from there. Blue lights caught her eyes, not the colors of Christmas; there must have been a car accident. This would be the winter of fender benders. The season of 2014 kept many body shops busy until spring.

She spotted the blue of Danny's hat coming toward her and breathed a sigh of relief. He hurried along through the crowded walkway; their eyes met before he reached the doorway.

"Hey Mom," he blurted out breathlessly, "Did you see the accident?"

"No, just the lights from the cruiser, and the stopped traffic."

As she spoke, the twosome headed in the opposite direction toward their car. Her thoughts now on more time lost. Ed would be waiting for them.

"Someone ran a stop sign, looks like. The other driver was really mad. The lady in the car said she couldn't afford to have an accident. The guy tried to calm her down. I think there were kids with her. Do you think anyone was hurt?" Dan went on excitedly. "The cars were really smashed up."

He was unable to stop chattering about the incident as they crawled over the snowbank and into their awaiting car.

"I heard it from inside the store. Even over the music. Ice. Everyone said it was an icy corner on Glendon Street and that it just keeps freezing up," Danny went on.

"Put on your seat belt," Kate ordered automatically.

She glanced over at her son and turned on the heater. She hoped she could drive past it all since she didn't know any other way out of town.

"Mom, you know the guy last summer- the one at the lake fest. He gave out free balloons?"

"Yes. I remember him," Kate paused absently as she turned off toward the old train station and tried to cut through a side street to avoid the site of the accident.

"Well, the guy in the accident looked just like him," Dan stated as a matter of fact.

Kate turned her head in his direction. He was very observant. She didn't say any more as they wound around the corner. The damaged cars were already being towed away, one sat in the lot of a local market. An ambulance too had just driven up. Police had cordoned off the area. Few people lingered in the cold, and Kate took a quick look. She could hear the sand and ice beneath her own tires, so she didn't hold her gaze long. Clearly, neither car was operative. She poked Dan and winked at him.

"Let's get out of town," she joked, glad to be on her way South.

Dan continued to stare back at the scene. Kate wondered if anyone had been injured. Sand was useless when ice kept forming, and black ice was impossible to identify. She gladly headed toward the highway. She had a fair to deliver to and a dance to attend. Anyone could get into an accident with such road conditions, especially in the dark. She would be glad to be closer to her destination.

Pulling out a brown bag from her purse, she pushed it toward Dan. It was hardly a decent meal, but it would have to do. It was a jelly donut and a small carton of milk. She fiddled with the radio and found another station playing holiday tunes. She wanted to put the accident out of her mind and began to hum along.

"I'll be home for Christmas," she sang.

Danny's mouth was too full of the donut to object. He rolled his eyes and carefully checked his purchase, pushing it deeper into the pocket of his jacket. He looked quite pleased with himself, Kate thought. He was getting to be quite a little man lately. He'd grown three inches that year.

They were soon on Route 93 South. It would be about an hour before they arrived on Pawtuckaway Lake. There was an entire week ahead of them. She let her mind wander. She hadn't been to a dance in years. It would be fun to participate in all the festivities coming up that night.

There was much ahead of them. The season had begun.

CHAPTER 33

"Santas Everywhere"

Ice and snow failed to dampen Christmas, even a disastrous storm, as it was called. The results of the November 26th snow were hardly a blip on the screen for the residents of Hampton Hills. No heat, no electricity, caved in roofs, water damage were all memories a month later as hearty New Englanders proved once more that not even a disaster could cloud their image of a proper celebration.

The parish priest had lost his nativity scene when the church roof collapsed and crushed it. It was an antique set, brittle, and irreplaceable. A parishioner arrived, built an elevated platform, and delivered their own set of figurines. They placed it just outside and nightly arrived to place a lantern next to it in the snow. No one objected that year about being politically incorrect.

Flooded floors in the chapel would have canceled all the town festivities had not a local carpenter arrived with his two sons and replaced all the wet boards. They polished the floors leading up to the alter, and refinished and stained the floor in the basement. A local roofer repaired the leaking tiles, patched it despite the frozen pieces, and promised to return in spring to replace the entire roof.

It wasn't long after that that the ladies of town marched in the back door of the church laden with pastries and handmade items. Tables quickly filled with woolen mittens, scarves, table runners, and hand painted ornaments, alongside carefully wrapped cookies, pies, and cakes. And just as quickly, residents arrived at the front door to purchase them.

The schedule would be adhered to. First the bake sale and crafts, then visits with Santa. The tables would be cleared and re-purposed for the dance, and a bar set up for drinks. All this would take place in the church basement. Fire department volunteers would move tables and serve as bartenders. Cocktails would be available by eight-thirty and dancing around nine. If you could have stood on the Island in the Sun on Pawtuckaway Lake, and peered inside the homes along its shores, the lakers could all be observed preparing for the evening celebrations.

Ed Shea's new jacket hung smartly on the closet door in his bedroom. His refrigerator was full of food for his daughter and grandson's visit. Wrapped gifts sat beneath his yet to be decorated tree. Another bag sat tucked behind an arm-chair with stocking stuffers and assorted smaller items. Ed was ready for the evening ahead.

Across the lake at the MacNamara camp, Meghan's tiny tree could be seen clearly from all angles. Ed glanced out and silently hoped they would have some time together over the next few days. He wanted to speak to her, even if he wasn't sure what he wanted say, or how to say it.

Inside the MacNamara camp, Max observed Meghan who seemed a bit agitated. He wore a red plaid bow that matched the pillows, candles, ribbons, and plates. A tree stood oddly in the corner of the room and he was not allowed to christen it. His bowls had been replaced with a wooden soldier, which did not guard his food as well as he did.

Meghan glanced over at the oatmeal cranberry cookies she had finished bagging, all tied with red ribbon. Blocks of fudge shone in red cellophane pack-aging. A large bowl of popcorn was set aside to become stale so they could finish decorating her tree when everyone had arrived.

Her refrigerator too was loaded with food: soda, wine, fruit, breads, pies, and cut vegetables. A large bowl of nuts sat on the table in front of the fireplace. She had meats and relishes for cold and hot meals. She felt ready to greet her guests.

Next door, Alice waved at Bob as he pulled out of the driveway, dispatched to deliver additional gifts for the visit with Santa. More children than usual had been invited this year. He would go to Mr. G's and collect clothes, candy, and pretty notebooks, dropping them by the church along with two trays of pastries. Members of Alan Shepard student council were there wrapping. Every child would receive a gift. Alice had added some scarves, stuffed animals, toys, and comfy blankets. Ed picked up some flying saucers for sledding. He would be back in about an hour. She headed in to take a bath.

In South Channel, Joe Moreau snuggled under a thermal quilt, coughing and sneezing. His beard had grown in perfectly this year: long and snowy white with just enough whiskers. Joe was proud to be the fair's official Santa. He wife, Rita, stood at the door of their bedroom, a look of concern on her face.

"Who do I call?" She asked him.

"I have to go," he answered in a weak voice.

"No one wants a runny nosed Santa," she said firmly.

"I can't cancel," he groaned from beneath the covers.

Rita tucked him in, removed the empty soup bowl from the bedside table, and turned off the light. She closed the door and headed for the kitchen where her phone was kept.

Her Santa was stuck in the North pole. Something had to be done. And quickly.

CHAPTER 34

"All Roads Lead to Town"

"Sorry, but Joe isn't going anywhere tonight," Rita Moreau explained to Alice Finch, "He has got a fever and sore throat."

Alice understood. She hung up the phone and flopped in a kitchen chair, still damp from her bath. Where would the Christmas committee get a replacement now? It was a busy season for them. Joe had been doing it for decades. He made the best one; the suit fit with little padding. Once he retired, they had often wondered, who could take it over? His brand was the real thing.

She picked up the phone to call the chairman. The call went to voice mail. She thought for a minute and redialed.

🌲 🌲 🌲

Danny and Kate hummed along, sang and chatted as they drove south on Route 93. Trees lined the highway, laced with icy frosting. Homes in surrounding towns resembled 'Currier & Ives' paintings. New Hampshire inspired holiday cards in its winter wonderland state. Kate knew that these winter trips would not last forever.

Danny was already too old for Santa, but the holiday continued to hold special magic for him. It was still all about the lake and grandpa. She held to this herself, as another fleeting stage to cherish, if she could. Parenting had its moments. This was one of them.

The exit came up sooner than she'd expected, and she was on Mountain Road. Under her tires was a layer of ice and sand. She slowed down. Plows had done their best, but the amount of base was like a ski slope. A look into the wooded areas reminded her of just how much of a dumping November had left behind. Black limbs held leaves that still clung to their branches, white with a coating of the frozen stuff. Many trees remained bent from the weight. Her car bumped along as she drove over frost heaves. It felt like an old washboard beneath her.

"Mum, Grand dad was really buried in snow, wasn't he?" Dan commented.

It seemed as if white dominated the scene for miles until the deep grayish edges of Pawtuckaway Lake peaked through the trees.

"We're here!" He yelled.

They pulled up behind the back porch. Max's large brown form appeared from nowhere and headed for the stopped car. Danny was out in seconds to greet him.

"What's Max doing over here?" He immediately wondered.

The three of them stepped up the sandy steps. Kate and Danny stomped their boots outside and then pushed opened the back door.

"Grandpa, we're here!" Danny sang out.

There was no response.

The house sat dark with only a light on over the kitchen sink. Christmas lights twinkled from the front windows to light her way, as Kate headed toward the front of the house. She looked out toward the shed and snowy yard. Still no sign of Ed. All sorts of crazy thoughts danced inside her head. She quickly shrugged them off and headed back toward the stairs leading upstairs.

"Anyone here?" She hollered up.

Again, she glanced toward the garage and noticed that the jeep was missing. Danny had already run upstairs and returned, confirming that Ed was not there.

Immediately, Katy hit the key on her cellphone for her father. She waited as it rang. Just as she was about to hang up, Ed's voice could be heard. It was very hard to hear him; he spoke in such a soft voice.

"Hi," he said.

"Hi, yourself," Kate replied still waiting for some explanation for his absence.

"Where are you?"

"We are at your camp. Where are you?"

"Long story. Can't talk now. I'm over at the church," he muttered as if under water.

"Want us to head over?"

"Yes. See you soon."

And with not another word, he hung up.

Danny sat on the couch facing his mother with a look of puzzlement on his face.

"What's up?" He asked while petting Max.,

"Grandpa is already over at the craft fair. He wants us to go there. Directly."

Danny watched his mother and detected no emergency. Kate shrugged and herded both the dog and her son back out towards the car. There had been some change of plans, so she would have to adjust. They rode in silence. Neither of them knowing what could have altered their plans. It was unlike Ed to act in such an impulsive way. Kate turned up the radio and hummed softly. Danny was too pleased to watch Max sitting like a passenger in the back seat to give the change of plans much thought.

All cars seemed to be heading toward the white spiral of the church. It had been dark for hours on this New Hampshire town. And as if to fend off the darkness, lights from windows and outside decorations directed them toward the celebration within. Since ancient times, mankind seemed to understand the need to use fire and light to draw people to one another. To her, the lit steeple of the church resembled a lighthouse that night. Even in stormy weather, the calmness of a single light gave one a feeling of a safe journey. Golden light poured out from the door to the church. The surrounding community would gather there. People walked in a single file, down the snow-edged sidewalks, in heavy boots and thick coats. She was suddenly delighted to be a part of it all.

Max leaned over from the back seat, and gave Dan a big kiss, as the boy and dog looked toward the white structure. Kate had to grip the steering wheel and force herself to focus on the road. She needed to park as close as she could, but the road was already lined with four-wheel drives. Finally, she spotted an opening and pulled in, glad to be off the icy road.

🌲 🌲 🌲

Voices squealed. Arms reached out. Packages were heard to crunch as the MacNamara family arrived at Clayton Shores. Meghan felt that Jimmy had grown two inches since the summer. Everyone admired the transformation Meghan had made in the camp. The place sparkled in red, green, and white.

"Where's Max?" Jimmy wondered.

"I'm not sure," Meghan admitted. "He was over at the Finches earlier but didn't come back."

"Maybe, he went out with the Finches for a ride," Beth proposed.

Kevin and Julie hustled their luggage into the last room down the hallway. Beth unrolled her sleeping bag on the floor beside her parents' bed, already planning on her space near the dog. While Tommy quickly headed up the stairs to the loft.

"When I am big, I want to sleep up there too," Beth commented. "But I get to sleep next to Max," she added with satisfaction.

The door opened and Ann arrived. Alone. She wasn't ready to spring a new beau on them quite yet. Mike would join them at the dance. He was staying in Manchester.

Ted and Peg would arrive in a few days. They planned to be there for New Years. Flying international involved more planning, and they hoped to remain into the new year. Meghan liked the idea of having more time to enjoy them all in shifts. Already the place felt crowded. But the laughter and excitement filled the rooms as everyone found a place for their things and started to consider what to do next.

Beth wanted to finish decorating the tree. Tommy wondered if there was a snow pile big enough to slide on. He had noticed a mound just up the road where the plow had circled and pushed the surrounding snow into one place. Questions about the upcoming events in town began. Meghan found it difficult to decipher which demand to act on first. And so, she stepped back and headed into the kitchen to make hot chocolate. With so many adults, why not just let them decide. She had a history of running a family, but it felt right to let it all fall into place by itself at that moment.

Suddenly, little Beth was standing beside her.

"I can do the whipped cream," she offered.

And so, the oldest and youngest found each other and prepared a warm drink with lots of chocolate, whipped topping, and marshmallows. Beth proved to be a master of the whipped cream can.

All roads would lead to town that night.

Beth was worried that Santa would never find them there deep in the New Hampshire woods. Tommy assured her, with his older brother wisdom, that with a chimney, it was easy. That was how he found most houses on Christmas eve. No one disagreed with his logic. Meghan and Ann put finishing touches on their hair while admiring the fancy clothes each had picked out for the evening. Kevin and Julie disappeared to the shed to hide presents, while the children sat in the kitchen, busy stringing soft popcorn. They would all leave soon to visit the town's North Pole workshop and have a chat with Santa.

Still concerned about Max, Meghan called the Finches.

"Is Max with you?" She asked into the answering machine.

She tried their cellphone but received no answer there either. Looking over toward her neighbors, she noticed that there were no inside lights on. Max was not left out in the winter. But it was not like him to wander either. She stepped out onto the porch and stood beside the small tree.

"Max. Max. Come," she yelled into the snowy darkness.

Danny wandered out and stood beside her.

"I like your tree," he said. "It has a pot like a plant."

"Yes. I will plant it in the ground in the spring," she explained as she ushered him back inside out of the cold.

She would leave the festivities if no one could tell her where Max was. But for now, they all needed to get ready and head there. The evening was already full of enough unknowns. She would adjust to each one at a time. The important thing was that they were all together.

CHAPTER 35

—◦—◆⦂◆—◦—

"Missing"

Kate and Danny carried Ed's special holiday birdhouses past tables of colorful ornaments and silver jewelry. Smells of maple syrup filled the air. The kettle corn popped gleefully in the corner sending more sweetness into the warm air. Neither had eaten much. Hot chili and hot dog signs invited them toward the kitchen door. But their eyes swept the crowded basement for Ed. They had left Max in the car and could not stay long. Dan had wrapped him in his own sleeping bag.

"Oh, yes. There you are. You can put them there," a friendly woman directed them.

Alice Finch came across the room looking distracted. Kate tried to get her attention. Motioning, she mouthed, "Where is my father?" Alice smiled, nodded, and pointed in the direction of what appeared to be the cloak room and continued off with purpose in her gait. Dan and his mother stood amid the moving crowd, puzzled. The tables were doing a smart business. Kate decided to eat something before they decided what to do next. They set off in the direction of the food signs and soon were munching on chili and hot dogs. They found seats that faced into the crowd, and quickly ate while keeping an eye out for Ed. A long line wound around the periphery of the room with toddlers awaiting their visit with Santa. He was hidden from view, but an elf continued to hand out small gifts to each child.

Kate noticed that there was a table displayed with silver jewelry and that the woman standing behind it was the real estate lady from the past summer. She had been engaged to the guy Danny thought he'd seen earlier in Wolfeboro. Kate thought that she had seen him up there before as well. Also, she recognized the hairdresser and the veterinarian's receptionist. It seemed that everyone in town was involved with the town's holiday events.

"We should buy another pie for later," Dan offered.

There was an entire table devoted to pies, tree shaped cookies, gingerbread houses, and breads just to the right of their seats. But as they finished off their bad diet of food, Kate decided to put off such a purchase. But it all looked so tempting to them both.

"There is the lady with the balloons," Dan said and pointed toward the sterling silver display.

"Yes. I noticed her before," Kate confirmed.

Stomachs full, it was time to decide what to do next.

Meanwhile, under the seat of her car, her cell phone was just recording a brief message from Ed. It had slipped from her coat pocket while they were busy tucking in their canine resident.

"Look. I'm helping a friend. Kind of last minute. Can't really talk. See you at the dance."

Ed's voice spoke to the dog. Max whined but dug deeper into the wonderful smell of a small boy, and quickly drifted off to sleep.

Kate reached into her coat pocket as they got up from the table. Her phone was gone. She could not call her father now. In her heart of hearts, she wondered if this favor of his involved a woman. She would not discuss this with Danny. All of this passed through her mind as she cleaned up their plastic utensils and napkins, and headed back to the car and their fury passenger. They needed to get home, get changed, and leave Max back in a warm house. It was all confusing, but there must be a logical explanation. It would be answered later. No use in letting her imagination go wild.

"We need to go home with Max and get changed," Kate said with more conviction than she felt.

"But where is grand dad?" Danny insisted

"I'm sure he will catch up with us."

As they settled into the car minutes later to an overjoyed dog, Kate could hear the blip of an unanswered message on her phone. It came from under her seat. She found her phone and pushed play. Relieved, she started her car up. But Bob Finch was standing at her car window . She rolled it down.

"Look. I'll take Max." His voice strained from breathlessness.

"I was going to bring him back to Dad's," she countered.

He looked over at Dan and winked at Kate. She was even more puzzled.

"He can come inside with me for a while. I am going back for something at the camp. I will drop him off at Meghan's," he explained.

"Have you seen my father?" She blurted out.

"Yes."

Again, he glanced over at her son.

"He's otherwise engaged. You will see him later at the dance, I'm sure." His eyes pleaded for her to not pursue this.

Kate opened the back door and Max jumped out. She watched them head back inside. *Why so many secrets*, she thought.

She headed back to the lake to unpack and dress for the dance, feeling only slightly relieved that no one except her seemed a bit worried about her father's whereabouts.

Still. Where *had* he been?

CHAPTER 36

———◆:◆——

"The Dance Begins"

Before the line of children, anxious to get Santa's ear, sparkly balls hung from the ceiling of the church basement. Musicians were tuning their instruments, and a singer fiddled with the sound system. Firemen dismantled craft tables and pushed them to the side. Teen girls covered each table with a white tablecloth, and sprinkled the surface with tiny snowflakes, placing a circle of white votive candles in the center. A long table was dragged to the corner where liquor bottles and glasses chinked, ice crunched, and the area became the official bar. Four men soon donned white shirts and black ties and jackets, ready to serve drinks.

Dozens of parents waited patiently in line, holding the hands of their children, because nothing could begin until each had had their visit, and told the bearded fellow their heartfelt wishes. He ho-hoed as best he could and listened intently. Phones flashed photos and young mothers cried. Like a three-ring circus, one act was just ending, and the other ready to begin. A few couples warmed up on the dance floor showing off their skills.

Meghan arrived with all the MacNamaras in tow. She and Ann could see that things were still transitioning into the evening. Alice Finch had been seen carrying the rest of the bake sale items back to tables, where they were cut up bite size for the dance. Bob Finch was spotted leaving the hall. Music began to fill the air. They took seats and filled their own long table in minutes.

"Sam will sit with us too," Meghan announced. "We'll save one for him," she added.

"We'll need an extra chair for Mike," Ann interjected.

The MacNamara women shone like new pennies. Their sequined tops and added bling reflected a bit of glamour usually reserved for New Year's Eve. Beth was one of the last in line for Santa. Kevin stood in line outside the North Pole and chatted with the elf.

Meghan and Julie awaited their photo opportunity. At first Beth resisted, but Santa seemed to put her at ease, and soon she started to chat with him. They felt they had a great picture of her. Tears filled Meghan's eyes. Beth was the last to believe in this magic. She wanted it all captured in her photo. A fleeting image of Sally appeared. Meghan had become a great advocate of taking photos since sorting the family album. This picture was a piece for the future.

Turning back toward their table, Meghan noticed that Ann's new interest had arrived. Ann stood beaming as she introduced him. Bob and Alice had also come over and attached an extra table to theirs. Alice looked a little tired but smiled broadly as they took their seats. The MacNamara gathering grew.

Beth had finished her visit with Santa and had been dropped off in the church nursery. The committee had seemed to have thought of everything. The Future Teachers of America from Alan Shepard High School offered movies, blankets, and games to their charges. This gave parents a chance to dance. The numbers would dwindle as the evening moved on and the little ones fell asleep; families would head out over the course of the evening. Bob and Alice chatted with the other ladies who had spent weeks reorganizing this series of events into a smooth weekend. Ann and Mike took to the dance floor spinning playfully together. Meghan could not restrain her happiness for her daughter and smiled at the sight. Kevin and Julie stood near the punch bowl, checking up on their daughter. Santa had disappeared and small voices sounded from the nursery. Satisfied that Beth was settled in with the others, they led one another onto the dance floor as well. Meghan noticed Tommy helping someone set up larger speakers. She wondered where Dan was. And where were Kate and Ed?

She stood up and walked toward the pastry table. She caught a glance at the musicians. There was no Ed among them. There was also no sign of Sam Norton. Her cell phone was in the pocket of her jacket; she refused to check it again. The night was young she told herself. She must be patient.

CHAPTER 37

———◦—◆‹◦›◆—◦———

"Dog Sitting"

Bob Finch brought drinks for everyone at the table. Kevin and Julie danced non-stop. The dance floor filled quickly with parents taking advantage of their time together. Alice and Meghan joined many others to do the 'Macarena' and the 'Greek line dance.' One women led them in a Western dance, in her white snake-skin cowboy boots. The music carried them away as they frolicked in the season. Meghan noticed that Kate and Danny had arrived. One of the firemen/ bartenders immediately led Kate onto the floor. She looked lovely in her black slacks and white shiny top. Dan found Tommy; the pair could be seen in the corner engrossed in a computer game. Ed Shea had not yet appeared. Kevin took his mother's hand and suddenly she was waltzing.

Everyone seemed engaged. Meghan found herself gazing at the empty seat she had saved for Sam. She headed for the punch bowl and stood sipping her drink. Her coat hung in the cloak room and she was tempted to go, find her phone, and check for new messages. Instead, she headed for the ladies' room to inspect her hair and lipstick. It was after ten, by the clock shining inside on the kitchen wall. She felt deflated. What was his excuse this time? Everyone had found their way here, except him. She needed a distraction. She wanted to leave and find Max. That was still bothering her and was a good reason to excuse herself early.

She passed by the door of the nursery and glanced in to peek at Beth. The toddlers were in a circle, giggling madly as they put the final touches of hat, scarf, and red coat on a co-operating dog. She stopped. The dog was her Max. What was he doing here? And who had brought him? Relieved and disappointed, she headed back to her seat. She had to wait. She had no good excuse to leave now. But Max had spotted her. In seconds, he leapt past the children, and headed toward Meghan. Beth followed squealing.

"Grandma! I just knew it was Max. He is a dog elf!" She announced.

The teens quickly subdued the dog. With Meghan's firm grip on his collar, the dog and crowd returned to the nursery to finish their project on him . Meghan waited until Max settled down and allowed them to place a set of red ribbons up his tail. She had to get back to the dance.

Someone had taken the microphone on the stage. The musicians halted and the hall became still. Meghan ducked into the restroom and glanced in the mirror. She smacked her lips and pushed some loose strands of hair behind her ears. She could not make out what the speaker was saying.

"That dog," she said aloud to her reflection in the mirror over the sink.

Not sure if she meant Max or Sam, she headed back to her seat.

CHAPTER 38

——❖——

"Found"

Deep among the woolen and down coats, muted by all the music and laughter, Meghan's cell phone beeped. His car was not drivable Sam said. He could not get a rental until the morning. He was unable to come to the dance. He was so sorry. But only the wood of the walls and plastic of the phone heard his story. His glass of champagne sat warm before a vacant seat. Meghan sat back with her family and the Finches. Santa appeared from behind the band and stood before the awaiting dancers. His white gloved hands took the microphone.

Meghan had to admit that Santa looked a bit askew. His beard had been shoved off-center. His hat appeared to be too small. He had lost weight. He waved to all those before him and then leaned in toward the microphone to speak. "Hello. It seems that I have failed to deliver one gift. There is something here…" His voice trailed off as he leaned down and appeared to be digging into his bag for something.

"Here it is," he announced.

This was unusual. One of the children must have gotten frightened and forgotten their present. Santa straightened his belt and his beard and slowly stepped off the stage walking toward the MacNamara's table. They wondered if Danny had not wanted to participate. Or was it Tommy who had failed to pick up a gift? The boys looked at one another puzzled.

But Santa stopped directly in front of Meghan. He extended his arms and placed a glistening red wrapped item on her lap. The oversized bow of green fell to one side. Everyone waited. She obliged him and carefully untied the bow. The paper fell open. Meghan held it up for the audience to see. It was her mother's birdhouse, the one missing from its limb since the storm had knocked it down. It had a new shiny copper roof and solid black floor. Her eyes began to tear.

"Dance with me," Santa whispered in her ear.

And as if on cue, the band began to play.

Alice grabbed Bob's hand. He whistled. Ann and Mike's eyes followed them as did most of the tables. In the center of the room, Meghan stood closely before a very red-bedecked Ed Shea, lost in the folds of his velvet suit and ample pillow-ing. Her son and daughter-in -law exchanged glances and joined in, still uncertain who this mystery man was in red. It was obvious to them all that Meghan seemed quite comfortable in his arms.

Someone dimmed the lights. Table emptied for the last dance. The musi-cians slowed down the tempo. An ocean of white created a ring around the man in red and his partner.

"Ed," Meghan finally managed to say, "you just disappeared."

"I was always here," he answered in her ear.

"You always have been," she replied.

"I always will be," he said and held her closer.

CHAPTER 39

"Loose Ends"

"Hey, it's Ted."

"How are you?"

"Good."

"I hear you and my sister are on again."

"Yeah, I think so. So, when are you coming over?"

"Not sure. Probably this week. Shooting for just after Christmas."

"Great." Ed struggled to proceed.

There was a pause as Ed sat down and fiddled with the folder in his hands. Ted waited.

"It's about the information I shared with you about Wil MacNamara. You asked me to wait. She plans to present all her findings to the family on Christmas eve. She hasn't said anything about Wil, so I assume that she has no answers. Isn't it time she found out what we know?" He sighed.

Across the Atlantic, Ted let his shoulders drop. Even from such a distance, Ed could see and feel his friend get that far off expression he would get when faced with a decision. He knew that suicide was not uncommon during the devastating years following 1929. This was one of the only facts that he had felt compelled not to share with Ed's sister. She was in a good place now, with Ed and all, he considered. But if not now, then when?

"Maybe, it is a good time to tell her what we know," Ted stated firmly.

Ed said nothing.

"Tell her when you find the right time. You will know. I trust your judgment. I think that Sally went through a lot of trouble keeping all this if she didn't plan to get to the bottom of it. And so many photos and journaling went in to creating a complete story. This is a piece of family history- if an unpleasant one," Ted added.

"And your mother, Sally, more than your father, wanted to preserve the story, despite Jack's efforts to let it go and keep his own boyish version alive."

Ed and Ted tried to justify their own decision.

The men moved on to discuss Ed's plans as the new year arrived. Ted wanted to find out if Ed was enjoying all his free time, and what was new on the lake. They discussed the availability of the airports in Manchester and Boston, and which would be the best option to get tickets during the holidays. Each one looked forward to seeing each other and bringing their families together. Like two high school pals they inquired about the Patriots and the Bruins. Ted admitted that it was harder to follow it all in England, and he missed the American sports coverage.

"I'm really happy that you and Meghan are together again," Ted repeated in closing.

"Thanks, me too. See you soon."

Ed placed the folder on the corner of his desk. He would include it among his food and assorted presents set aside for Christmas eve. He would find the opportunity before she presented her finished album. He would have to play it by ear.

Meghan had finally spoken to Sam the day after the dance. He was all apologies, explaining the extent of his car accident, his difficulty in tracking down a rental car, and how he had tried to contact her the night of the dance. Hadn't she received his text message? She listened.

"I'll be down for Christmas," he assured her.

"My family is here, with more to come at the end of the week. I have all sorts of plans …and obligations." She found herself saying in response. "Tommy and Beth have ski lessons in Manchester at McIntyre Ski Area and plans to ice skate at the JFK arena another day."

Sam felt like he was getting the brush off and didn't know why. There was plenty of time left to rendezvous. It was only December 21st, he insisted. He would make it up to her.

But Monday allowed Meghan to think. The camp was quiet, with most off to do some last minute shopping. She had her trays out to make Chex Party Mix, a family favorite. Between each batch, she toyed with her album. She felt pleased with the outcome. It held years of memories.

Between those pages, she had consolidated information she'd found in the words of Jack MacNamara's mother, Agnes. Among the photos and writing, Meghan had glimpsed into her father's childhood. She had observed their lives through Agnes' camera lens. Meghan was allowed behind the lens and into the struggles of being a mother before and after 1929, when life in one Manchester family would be altered forever. Only recently, had Meghan found the right words to insert into her album from none other than Ansel Adams:

"You don't make a photograph just with a camera.

You bring to the act of photography all the pictures you have seen, the books you have read, the music you have heard, the people you have loved."

What could explain Agnes' work of pictures better than such a quotation?

Her mother, Sally, had chronicled as much of the material that her mother-in- law had provided and set it aside for future inquiry. Letters, postcards, news clippings, personal observations were all intricate details of the MacNamara fabric. Jack MacNamara had to live with the unanswered question of what happened to his father; she would now be able to tie up the loose ends. Sally had wanted it done. Agnes had left so many breadcrumbs to follow. Surely, Meghan had come to Pawtuckaway Lake to complete the tale. And she had.

The most unexpected piece to this months-long journey came when Olive Smith added her unexpected revelation. Uncle Gerry was her key witness. As much as Wil's death was tragic, it had not been intentional. Gerry confirmed that an act of courage was the cause. Wil was heading home. He didn't make it, not from desperation, but rather from an unforeseeable accident. He had saved another's life. The official evidence was wrong. But it too would remain a part of Wil's story. Meghan felt that the women before her had collected and stitched her a quilt. She had only to sew on the edging. The final work of art was complete.

Christmas Eve was just days away. Pawtuckaway Lake was coated in dark gray ice. A full moon shone across its face. Ed Shea stood in the cold on its shore. He looked across and could make out the tiny tree lit on Meghan's deck. The lake held so many secrets beneath its solid surface. One of them would be revealed soon.

He would be glad to have the truth out. He had another truth to reveal to Meghan. It was good that he would now have the chance to tell her much that was in his heart. Timing was everything. Things were poised in his life. This would be one of the best Christmases ever.

He pushed his hands deeper into the pocket of his down jacket, feeling the package safely tucked inside.

CHAPTER 40

"Wrapped Gifts"

It was Christmas eve. Awaiting its moment, the tome sat in the center of the bed framed by one of Sally's quilts. Meghan had written a thesis in college and felt as if this was also a body of work worthy of research. Her family had proven to have a truth to prove, and she had succeeded in reveal an enormous one. The entire MacNamara story had finally been told.

She had wrapped it in plain brown, using four brown paper bags. Simple twine wound around its ample middle; her bow was a small branch from a pitch pine tree with two tiny pine cones still attached. A sprig of mistletoe topped the package. Meghan felt that the love stories captured inside reflected her completed work. It was Christmas Eve and never had she felt closer to all whom the album contained.

Agnes' heart lead her to Will and their family of boys. Sally had followed their son, Jack MacNamara, to the lake adding their own two offspring. Meghan MacNamara had returned decades later with her own brood, like a fish to the spawning ground, carrying all that came before with her. Soon most of her loved ones would assemble here. The family story continued to move forward.

Meghan folded the red corduroy slacks she intended to wear. She could hear the others as they hollered to one another over the sound of Christmas melodies. They wrapped gifts, cooked, showered, and dressed for the upcoming evening. Above it all was the high pitched voices of children excited about the presents to come. She straightened out her green Aran sweater running her index finger over the many patterns it held.

Didn't every Irish mother wish she could wrap her family inside a handmade sweater to protect them from the rough waters of life? Once again, she sat before the mirror and lined up the photo of Sally and Jack to reflect back to her as if they were sitting beside her. She held up the knitwear and pointed to the designs. The honeycomb pattern represented hard work— busy as a bee in order to succeed. A wide cable stitch ran up on both sides, and along the buttons of her sweater. Other hands had closed those eyelets and she felt them as she put the sweater on and secured the front. That stitch was said to represent the ropes of the fisherman's nets. Safety and a good catch were their hope for the one who wore it. For centuries, Irish women handmade these warm pieces of clothing. Meghan noticed for the first time the large diamond shape running along the sleeves. They stood for wealth and success. She thought more about all this as she cuffed the sleeves and tied a plaid scarf around her neck.

Meghan opened the curtain and stood before the lake. A full moon ran across, ending on her beach. Only in winter did the lake create a solid field of ice on which you could extend your land and walk. Lights flickered from houses along the opposite shore, no doubt its inhabitants hanging stockings and laying out food for family and one special nocturnal visitor.

She was stalling. She had only a few more minutes to herself. On her right wrist was the silver cuff Sally had given her. She held up her left hand, her wedding band no longer there. Ed had presented her with a pair of diamond and ruby earrings over dinner that week; they sparkled from each ear. He seemed to have won her heart.

She lifted her brown paper package and held it to her chest. She looked back at the mirror.

"Tonight, we are all together," she said to Sally and Jack.

She smiled and headed down the hall, wrapped in all that represented her own Irish family history.

CHAPTER 41

"Packages Delivered"

Ed Shea stood outside the door of the MacNamara camp. The driveway was already full of unfamiliar cars. It was Christmas eve. He could feel the weight of his two deliveries from inside the folds of his winter coat. He also felt a charge of electricity standing beside the small lit evergreen that greeted them that special night. He could hear voices and music coming from inside. He knocked and opened the door. Faces shone from the lit room; they looked up to greet him. A fire burned warmly from the fireplace. He noticed a collection of stockings hanging from the mantelpiece, and for a split second remembered his own dreams of childhood wonder. Max greeted him with an extended paw.

"Hey, my boy. Like the ribbon," he said softly to the canine.

"Ed, Merry Christmas. Good thing Max can't talk. He watched us dress you in red the other night. He seems to think that he has three houses to call his on this lake now," Bob said teasingly as he took his friend's coat.

"I should have known something was up when he went missing," Kate piped in.

Meghan reached for Ed's scarf and gloves and tucked them inside his sleeves. She'd grabbed the coat from Bob and headed for the bedroom down the hall to add it to the growing pile on the bed. Bob saw his opportunity and followed her.

The kitchen table and coffee table were covered with all kinds of goodies. Ed glanced at it all and smiled over at Kevin who sat on the couch with Beth, Tommy, and Julie. Kevin stood.

"Ed, can I get you a drink?" He offered.

"Yes, I'll be right back."

Meghan laid Ed's black pea jacket carefully at the end of her bed. She turned to find him standing awkwardly in the doorway. He had something in his hands.

"I need a minute alone," he said and closed the door.

The moment felt oddly intimate. Meghan held her breath. She stood still and then moved the coats to the side and sat. She indicated that he might join her there. Instead, he took only one step inside and pulled an envelope from his pocket.

"I have something to tell you," he began, "It pertains to Wil MacNamara."

"You knew?" Meghan immediately asked.

"Knew what?" Ed responded.

"You first," she answered.

"No. You go."

Ed pushed it back inside his back pocket and decided to sit.

"I spoke to Olive Smith at the library," Meghan began, "It seems that Wil was suspected to have committed suicide."

"Yes. That was what the newspapers reported."

Ed wasn't breathing.

"It doesn't, in any way, diminish the story you have compiled," he added softly.

"No. Someone else was there at the time and told a very different story," Meghan began again.

Ed looked at the woman before him and bit his lip. What other version he wondered? But he was so unwilling to blurt out the facts as he knew them that, again, he would not speak until he had heard her out.

"Olive knew a woman, Violet, who's uncle was also on the road riding the rails. He knew Will MacNamara. And according to his evidence, Wil died trying to carry another man safely across a trestle. He himself did not survive and must have jumped too late, hit his head on the way down, and was washed downriver by the currents. That is why Wil was later found in the Merrimack river. It all looked like suicide, but in fact, her uncle told a very different story about his untimely death. He was heading home, just never made it."

Ed Shea was never so happy to hear something in his life. He was the one with the incomplete story. Wil MacNamara would remain the man Jack wanted him to be, and his family would soon find out the entire reason for his disappearance. He pushed the envelope full of news clipping deep into his back pocket, and sat down hard against it.

There was a knock on the door. Ed and Meghan looked up. Kate stuck her head in, arms full of coats. With one glance, she closed the door and carried her load across the hall to the other bedroom.

"There is something else," Ed began.

Meghan did not want any more. She wanted her happily ever after. She did not want Ed to add anything that might jeopardizes this. Not tonight.

"Can it wait?" she mumbled.

"I don't want to wait any longer," Ed said as he stood before her.

He pulled her to her feet and held both shoulders. Then he reached inside his vest pocket and pulled out a small velvet box.

"Marry me," he said.

There was a moment's pause. Meghan finally exhaled. They both did.

"Yes."

CHAPTER 42

"The Final Opus"

(December 27-28, 2014)

Hampton Hills had canceled their holiday parade; the main street was simply too full of snow and ice, for marchers and their musicians to safely pass. Ed Shea was consulted by the new principal to see if such a thing had occurred before and what he had done to quell the disappointment among students, parents, and townspeople. He suggested an indoor concert in the high school gym. And so, the following weekend, most of Hampton Hills assembled again as a community to fill the stands.

Students reserved special seats for the ladies from the church who had worked so diligently to create the dance and bake all the food, offering soft drinks, cookies, and popcorn free to all attendees. Everyone seemed to enjoy themselves. Ed sat proudly next to his fiancé. Young teenage girls giggled that the principal had found a new wife despite his 'advanced' age. Their parents had other opinions, some remembering when both Ed and Meghan were young staff members years before.

As the gym filled with the sound of music, Ed's mind wandered as he sat in his school again. He thought of the folder and photo involving Sam Norton. He had birth records, visual evidence, and strong proof of Sam's relationship and resulting son. He had burned his copies. He saw no point in relating it all to Meghan. He was too proud and happy to bother with any of that now. It was all in the past in his mind.

Ann and Mike spent much of their school vacation in Boston. They drove north and did some skiing, visiting North Conway, one of the other *Christmas* towns in New Hampshire. They too seemed to be getting more serious. The family was delighted with the turn of events for Meghan and Ed. Mike had given Anne a gold bangle bracelet; she had not taken it off since Christmas eve.

Meghan looked as if she had won the lottery, as she sat once again in the gym of Alan Shepard High the day of the concert. She was back to the school where she had briefly taught; just down the hall was her old room. But she was not that girl. And she finally knew it.

Sam had called her repeatedly the past week. She'd remained quiet about the turn of events. The ruby and diamond ring glinted under the gym lights. She would soon be Mrs. Ed Shea. The events back in her young life felt long ago Ed's shoulder rubbed against hers as he lifted his arm to waved at another passing student. She felt much more a part of a life than a school staff; the school represented her future with its principal, but it did not include Sam Norton anymore.

Meghan later declined Ed's invitation to go out after the concert. With all her company gone, she suddenly felt the need to be alone. There were a lot of things to settle in her mind. They kissed when she asked him to drop her off. They embraced warmly then Meghan opened the jeep door.

"Talk to you tomorrow," he said as she kissed him again and stepped from the passenger seat.

Minutes later she was back outside with Max. He had been cooped up during her absence and needed some exercise. She tossed his favorite blue ball and watched him run after it and return it to her feet. The name 'Golden Retriever' really felt appropriate in moments like this; he loved to fetch.

The entire week had been so full. It was now the time to settle into the winter season. It would be her first one spent on the lake. She felt ready to embrace its offerings of ice skating and cross country skiing. Ed wanted to do more snowshoeing and offered to teach her the ropes. He seemed to enjoy coming over to visit both her and the Finch's on skies. She smiled at the thought.

Gifts were stored. There would be a bonfire with the Christmas trees. Bob and Alice agreed to make a unified trip to the dump with all the extra paper from gift wrap and meals. Meghan had begun to strip the beds of soiled flannel sheets and to launder towels. She would like a warm, windy day to air out her quilts. But what enveloped her that moment was a deep sense of peace, happiness, and completion.

Max had had enough. She emptied her pocket of dog treats and headed back into the camp. Looking at the shiny tree on her porch, she was pleased that it could stay there. It was after all in a plant pot. She looked forward to planting it in the ground. Somehow, in all the business, she had forgotten about it. And no one had yet claimed responsibility for it.

She wondered if the mail had come. Since she was in her outdoor clothes, she passed the porch and headed out toward the road to check the mailbox. After all the holiday sales, mail in January was quite scant. She opened the front and reached inside. A small white envelope sat leaning against the back of the metal container. She reached inside and pulled it to the front. Gripping it in her thick mitten, she glanced at the handwriting but didn't recognize it. Neither did she see any return address on it. Who would have left it she wondered? She did notice that it was addressed to 'Mrs. Meghan MacNamara O'Reilly.' She seldom saw her name written out like that.

Once inside, Max headed straight for his water bowl before stretching out on the braided rug in the living room. Meghan removed her coat and hat, and tossed her mittens into the glove basket still set up from her week with her grandchildren. She pulled out a butter knife and sat at the table, slitting the top of the envelope.

The enclosed card depicted a green tree with a red cardinal sitting on one branch. She read the enclosed message:

Dear Ms. Meghan,

I have been laid up with a bad ankle sprain and so have been unable to get around. Me and my wife missed out on all the town festivities this year. However, we had plenty of company down from Canada.

By now, you must wonder where your Christmas tree came from.

And why.

This is your first Xmas as a resident on our lake. I have traditionally delivered a fresh balsam fir, still in its roots, to my new customers. Your father and mother received one many years ago. But for those of us of Canadian descent, the evergreen tree is much more than an ornament. My grandfather was a victim of the 1917 Halifax Explosion. He lost his eyesight. Americans rushed to our rescue with aid. We will never forget their immediate response to the tragedies of that day.

Boston may get the largest tree we can send in appreciation, but a small tree on one small lake in New Hampshire is my way of remembering.

Welcome to Pawtuckaway Lake!

Looking forward to seeing you in the new year.

Signed,

Pete Levesque

Handyman

(plumber/ carpenter& other assorted jobs)

Meghan suddenly felt the tears, that she didn't know she needed to shed, begin. They were warm and wet, and rolled slowly down both cheeks. So much to know. So much to take in. The lake held so many stories. Even her album was unable to embrace them all. Right down to her tiny tree.

Meghan sat before her computer and prepared an email:

Dear Sam,

You will be seeing my engagement announcement soon in the paper. I truly enjoyed revisiting old times and reminiscing.

But I am in an exclusive relationship now. I wish you only the best.

I hope the Big lake is as good to you as Pawtuckaway Lake has been to me.

—Meghan.

Over the next few months, Bob and Alice invited Ed and Meghan over for many occasions. The winter was full of friends, food, and snow. Ed was seen often crossing the icy lake wearing a very red stocking hat. Max would spot him and announce his arrival long before he reached the opposite shore. Sally's birdhouse found a new branch. From Meghan's window over the kitchen sink, she frequently caught the glint of sun as it was reflected on the shiny copper roof.

Another season had begun for the residents of Pawtuckaway Lake. And a date would soon be selected for a spring wedding.

EPILOGUE

---•◆:◆•---

January 2015

Alice Finch stood before her sink absently washing out her coffee cup. The design on it was her favorite: Blue Willow. She had loved it since she was a child and had a shelf full of assorted pieces she'd collected over decades of yard sales and Goodwill browsing. Some pieces were lined with surface cracks. The design had been altered little over generations. She treated them like they were jewels.

Bob had given her a new corkscrew in her stocking. Such a silly tradition they kept. She wiped it dry and opened the drawer beside the sink where she kept other can openers and nutcrackers. The new wine opener had been carved with the 'Old Man of the Mountain.' It stared back at her, a symbol of wisdom, independence, and certainty. For perhaps 12,000 years, it was believed, its profile overlooked New Hampshire. Poets wrote about it. Statesmen defined the Yankee character by its stern face. Then on May 3rd, 2003, it fell to the ground. Mother nature created it and she destroyed it.

Pushing it inside the drawer, she eyed the velvet cover of her Rune cards.

"Not this time," she said aloud.

Also stashed in this drawer were the unopened letters she had been collecting since last October. The return addresses told her what they pertained to: her family estate. There was one from the law office, her brother, her sister, and an old family friend. Each one contained advice, requests, details, and information for her. She had put it all off until the new year. And the new year was here.

Naomi LaFrance, Alice's mother, had died the previous year. Alice found herself suddenly reminded of the wine opener. Her mother had such an expressionless face. Maybe that was how she kept her youthful looks over the years. Although everyone suspected she had had cosmetic surgery from time to time. Again, nothing could keep 'the Old Man' from disintegrating. Time ran out on Naomi too.

But what Alice could not fathom was why *she* had been chosen to settle the estate. Why not her older brother? He was far more methodical than she was. Or just let the lawyer do it. Mother and daughter were like oil and water. They had a lifetime of conflict. Naomi was never pleased with Alice's choices and was not quiet about her disapproval. Even dead, Naomi had a hand in the settling of the LaFrance legacy that Alice wanted nothing to do with. So why leave it all for her to direct?

Alive pulled the collection of sealed letters out. She wanted to burn them. There was no way out of it. She had to go to the coast and begin to eliminate and disperse personal items from the beach house. It had sat empty now for months. The caretaker had called periodically to report on snow removal and utility bills, but little could be done without her permission. She knew that her siblings wanted specific things. She knew that they wanted to sell it quickly. She also knew from a lifetime of Naomi that the will had its own plans. And she would soon know what the hand from the grave had predetermined.

Alice opened the drawer and shoved the envelopes further inside. She pulled on her winter coat. Six plastic tubs of Christmas decorations awaited storage in the back of Bob's shed. Finally, warm sun had made it possible for her to carry her holiday packages on a clearer path. Bob and she had carefully packed all her treasured items in tissue, and purchased smaller, more portable tubs. With his wrist still a little weak, she was the one to lug them out this year.

The holidays had been especially enjoyable for her. Meghan and Ed were engaged. The community of Hampton Hills had celebrated with more enthusiasm than she could remember. All the snow made it wintrier and cozier. Their little piece of heaven on Pawtuckaway Lake had truly experienced a special season. Why ruin it with all this upheaval from the past?

It could not be avoided.

She carried the first tub. As she returned for the second, she thought about her years of difficulty with her mother. Naomi was not the mother for her. Alice could not have been more different. Nothing Alice did was enough. Alice was a difficult teen, unhappy wife, and rebellious daughter in Naomi's eye. This life with Bob had taken many years to find.

She was on her last trip when she heard the cry of a seagull. It flew low over the frozen lake. A wind wound itself around the pine trees with the sound of an ocean tide. Could she smell salt air?

The last tub fit nicely in the far corner of the workshop. Alice closed the wooden peg on the front door and headed toward her house. Christmas was over. She could no longer focus on other people's lives. It was time she faced her own demons. The new year had begun, and decisions had to be made. She needed to go East. The LaFrance estate called out like a siren to her unwilling ears.

She must leave her lake home and spend some time at the seashore.